The Anthology-
Our Power

Dedication

To Monique,

"Mo" as I call you, thank you for being such a beautiful light in my life. Your friendship is a gift that I cherish deeply, and I am beyond grateful for the countless conversations, the laughter, and the moments of wisdom you've shared with me. Our long talks have been a source of comfort, inspiration, and strength, and I treasure every one of them.

You are the epitome of grace—always moving through life with kindness, warmth, and a heart full of love. Your sweet spirit and unwavering support mean more to me than words can express. I am truly blessed to know you, to call you a friend, and to have your presence on this journey.

With love and appreciation,

Kebra

Trigger Warning!

This anthology contains themes of gun violence, molestation, and other sensitive topics. Reader discretion is advised

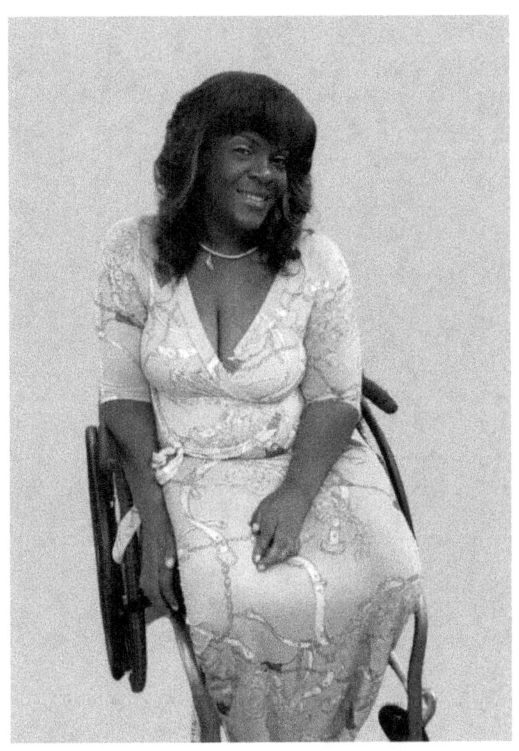

Monique Stamps, Contributing Author

Disability Advocate, Podcaster
Outreach Coordinator, Raw Beauty Project
Program Director, Women Embracing Abilities Now-Charlotte

No Fear of Depth

Introduction

"I must be a mermaid. I have no fear of depths but a great fear of shallow living." Anaïs Nin's words embody the woman I've become on my journey as a Black, disabled woman.

From my earliest memories, I've felt a connection to the sea and its mysterious mythical mermaids. Bath time and swim lessons were a playground for our imaginations. My siblings and I brought scenes from *Jaws* to life, hosted Barbie pool parties in post-rain mudholes, and transformed into mermaids when my sister and I took to the water! *Splash,* starring Daryl Hannah, is one of my favorite movies, while *The Little Mermaid* is my sister's favorite. Every chance we got to swim, we pretended to be mermaids. We loved the way our hair looked when wet, our curly afros transforming into wavy, mermaid-like tresses that cascaded down our backs as we emerged from the pool, then returned back into our curly puffs when dry made us feel magical.

Our parents took my sister, my brother, and two first cousins on my mom's side to the beach with us almost every summer. Each time our family car neared the ocean; my heart would race as the salted air and the scent of ocean life filled my senses. I'd roll down the window to take deep breaths of the nautical breeze. My dad, a former lifeguard and an excellent swimmer, shared a deep love for the ocean, which became one of very few things that we had in common, besides the fact that I had his entire face.

While he spent most of his time fishing from the pier, he also played in the waves with my siblings and cousins. The ocean was our safe haven, filled with some of our best memories of him. But he always reminded us of its dangers, especially the rip currents. He taught us how to stay calm if caught in one—how to relax, avoid swimming against it, and instead move parallel to the shore.

I remember one time, swimming far out from where my dad stood knee-deep in the water, fishing. I swam back toward him but suddenly lost my sense of direction. I couldn't tell which way was up or down or whether I was being pulled out or in. I felt myself being carried by the current and remembered my dad's advice: stay calm, don't fight it, and just go with the flow.

I let the water guide me, and eventually, I felt myself being pushed. Then, I bumped into something—soft, fleshy. Suddenly, I popped to the surface, and there I was, right next to my dad.

"Girl, that current could've taken you away," he said, shaking his head. "You better be glad it swept you back this way."

I told him I stayed calm, just like he'd taught me. But deep down, I felt there was more to it. Something—or someone—guided me back to safety. Call me crazy, but I believe it was an ancestor or a mermaid, Yemayá the Yoruba Queen Goddess of the sea.

Becoming a Mermaid

I was born in Chester, SC and raised nearby on a dirt road in rural Rock Hill, surrounded by family, our family businesses, and our farmland. As a little girl, I loved being able to walk to my great granddad's store to get Chico-Sticks, Now & Laters, and Pickled Sausages, then run down to my granddad's and uncle's auto shop to be nosy and get a cold glass bottle Dr. Pepper (I don't know why but the Dr. Pepper's from the shop tasted so crisp and extra cold). Then I would run up to my cousin's fish store just to say hi or if my grandma told me to buy something. I hated the smell of fish and refused to eat anything that came out of the water. It's still true till this day, as in my mind I'm a mermaid, I can't eat my people!

I was a tall, statuesque beauty with long, thick hair and legs as long as Highway 72, where our two-story red house stood. I enjoyed living in the country visiting neighbors and hearing back in the day stories from the elders and holding on to lessons learned from them to carry with me into adulthood. My next-door neighbor, Freddy, was paralyzed from the neck down from a car accident when I was about 8 years old.

My mom was a registered nurse and often helped him and his family whenever they needed her. I loved to go with her and would help him, too. I used to visit on my own just to talk to him and help with simple things like feeding him or giving him water. I remember how handsome and tall he was. His voice was so deep and powerful that he could have narrated audio books or been on the radio. I think he did radio for a short time at a Christian station before he passed later in life when I was in college. As I grew into a teenager, I continued to help Freddy while living my life figuring out how to get to my big city dreams from the limited reach from the country.

I loved fashion and had a natural talent for hair and makeup. I drew inspiration from icons like Linda Evangelista, Cindy Crawford, Iman, Tyra Banks, Grace Jones, and makeup artist Sam Fine. I dreamed of becoming a fashion model, a celebrity stylist, or both. I was also musically inclined. I played piano and sang in church and for family from time to time. I was too shy to pursue music as a career unless I was singing or playing keys as backup. My creativity, gifted hands, and beauty were going to make me rich—or so I thought.

On March 25, 1995, my dreams came crashing down. That morning, my mom insisted on stopping my sister and me to pray before school. We whined about it, worried about being late, but reluctantly held hands and let her pray. Then we headed out in my tiny white Geo Metro, a car I always thought looked like a Tic Tac—and one I felt too tall for.

That day, the usual road to school was under construction, so I took an alternate route. Little did I know the new road had fresh jackhammered pavement with no warning signs. As my car climbed a curved incline, it suddenly sank into the uneven road. The Geo Metro fishtailed, slid as if it was on ice, and violently flipped five times into a freshly plowed field. My classmate, still on a tractor nearby, saw the whole thing.

When the car finally stopped upright, the smell of gas, blood, smoke, and broken glass filled the air. My sister was standing at the driver's side door, terrified. I asked her to pull me out, but she hesitated, recalling what our nurse mother had taught us — never move someone after an accident to avoid worsening injuries. But the fear of the car catching fire pushed me to beg her to help.

She cried, begging me not to die as blood dripped from her head. My classmate and his dad rushed her home to get my parents and called 911. Lying on the soil, I felt cold, as if something heavy pressed on my chest. But I remained calm, sensing an otherworldly peace.

A blue car stopped, and a white woman in scrubs with a wavy bob approached me. She said, "Honey, I'm on my way to work, but I saw your car and had to stop." When I told her I was freezing, she brought a blanket from her car, wrapping me gently. "I hate to leave you," she said, "but I have to get to work."

Her warmth and care reassured me. I then felt God's presence sweep across my face. I knew, no matter what happened, I would be okay. When my family and EMTs arrived, they removed the blanket, and I immediately felt cold again. I told them about the nurse, but they insisted there had been no blanket on me when they arrived with puzzled looks on their faces as they cut my clothes off me. Could she have been an angel sent to comfort me while I was in the field alone?

I knew then that my life had changed forever. As I was airlifted to Carolinas Medical Center, I understood I would never walk again. It was confirmed; I had broken my neck at C $4/5$ level. I was a quadriplegic. I had become a mermaid.

Navigating New Waters

After spinal fusion surgery and four months of inpatient therapy, I attempted to return to high school in person but eventually finished at home. I spent the next year and a half in outpatient therapy, learning how to navigate daily life and regain as much independence as possible.

Friendships faded as people struggled to adjust to my new reality. Some didn't know what to say or do, while others simply drifted away. Disability wasn't normalized then the way it is today, so I didn't blame them—they were kids, too, figuring out life after high school.

I also dealt with constant visitors from church, praying for me, trying to stand me up, or dragging my heavy body across the floor. People kept telling me, "God said you'll walk again," or "I had a dream that you were walking." I'd roll my eyes, thinking, *"Well, I think God would run that information by me first."* I appreciated their intentions but knew they were wrong. Most of the time it felt like bullshit, just something to say to make them feel better or prove their prophetic gift. A few years later, when I was in college, I made the mistake of letting a stranger pray for me and the fool snatched me clean out of my chair in the "NAME OF JESUS!!!"

My life was saturated with healing. People calling at 3am praying, Mom taking me to a healing service of one of the biggest pulpit pimps in Christianity, that damn Benny Hinn! *TBN* and *700 Club* on my screen 24/7 with these weird white preachers and white Jesus was driving me to bitterness towards "the church," so much so that I started my journey to deconstructing from Christianity as it was fed to me.

I have never allowed anyone to "lay hands" and pray for me again. God had already given me peace about my disability, and I wished others would stop viewing me as something broken that needed fixing and accept it as I had.

Determined to rebuild my life, I focused on independence and self-discovery. Case managers tried to push me into day programs and sheltered workshops, but I refused. Those environments weren't for me, and I wasn't afraid to say so—even if it meant clashing with professionals who didn't see my potential.

With the support of a vocational rehabilitation counselor, I enrolled at Winthrop University in 1997 to study social work. I learned to drive a modified Ford Econoline van with a lift and hand controls, giving me newfound freedom. During my internship with the Chester County School District, I mentored high school girls with disabilities that reinforced my passion for advocacy.

In December 2001, I earned my Bachelor of Social Work degree. But the post-9/11 economy and lingering discrimination against people with disabilities made finding a job in my field challenging. I took a part-time administrative role with the City of Rock Hill, shredding more paper than I could stand, but I knew I was destined for more.

I finally got a dream of a job at the Center for Independent Living (CIL) in Charlotte, NC, in 2004 as a Peer Mentor and disability rights advocate. I wanted to be a voice for women and girls with disabilities, helping them see their worth and potential. In 2010, I discovered Janice Jackson, Founder of Women Embracing Abilities Now (WEAN) in Baltimore, a mentoring program for women with disabilities. Janice blessed me with an opportunity to start a chapter of WEAN at the CIL, who agreed to be fiscal sponsor of the program. This was my calling, Yemayá was guiding me further into the waters, deeper into my purpose.

Knee Deep

In 2003, I became pregnant with my first child, my daughter, Camryn. The reactions to my pregnancy were... memorable, to say the least. They ranged from joy and excitement to fear, judgment, ignorance, and even moments of unexpected humor.

One acquaintance's mother, for instance, jumped to a startling conclusion. She asked her daughter who had raped me. In her mind, that had to be the only explanation. After all, who would willingly have a child with a woman in a wheelchair? A woman who is beautiful, college-educated, drives, is of sound mind, and fiercely independent? It was as if my capabilities and my humanity were invisible to her.

Then there was my sweet Aunt Arlener, who called me after hearing the news. Her voice was filled with genuine joy as she told me what a blessing my pregnancy was. But she didn't stop there. In a hushed tone, she whispered something I'll never forget: "Well, niece, I didn't know you could spread your legs!"

On the flip side, one reaction left a deep scar. A close friend, someone I trusted, responded to my joyful announcement with words that stung. Her tone carried judgment, jealousy, and disappointment as she asked, "Why would you do that?" Her words cut deeper than I expected, overshadowing the happiness I'd hoped to share.

Those moments taught me a lot about people, their assumptions, their biases, and their inability to see past their own limitations. Through it all, I held on to the joy of bringing Camryn into the world. She was, and always will be, my greatest blessing.

My mom told me, "You live life like you don't have a disability." Well, that's the point of it all for me. I know that being paralyzed from the chest down, not having finger dexterity and not being able to walk comes with many challenges in life that I've learned to navigate through differently, and I still have every right to live life as I chose. I'm still me. I have figured out things so far. I knew I would be a great mom!

The medical care I received during my pregnancies was vastly different. With Camryn, my OBGYN in Rock Hill, SC, had an incredible attitude and excellent bedside manner. However, the physical accessibility of the medical diagnostic equipment posed significant challenges, making it difficult to receive proper prenatal care. On top of that, I had an unfortunate encounter with a cruel "paycheck" nurse.

While alone in the birthing room, she informed me they needed to move me to a regular room. When I explained that I was paralyzed and needed assistance transferring, she flatly refused to help or call for assistance. Instead, she threatened to call security. Stunned and unsure of what to do, I took my time and eventually managed to get myself into my wheelchair. I didn't tell anyone what happened, I chose to keep the peace and limit my stress for Camryn's sake.

Just eight days after Camryn was born, I survived a post-eclampsia stroke. The stroke's severity, compounded by subsequent seizures, left me with a neurodivergent brain. I don't remember anything from that day. I was told my blood pressure was 240/120. My mouth twisted and I called for my baby girl as if I was bargaining with God to let me stay here for her. I was in and out of consciousness for weeks. The stress leading up to it had been immense, finding out at nine months pregnant that the love of my life, my high school sweetheart, was married and already had a child, combined with the awful treatment from that "paycheck" nurse, had been too much for my mind and body.

I have a tendency to hold things in, to push through without addressing wrongdoing in the moment—for both my own sanity, and quite honestly, the offender's safety. I held my peace as much as I could, knowing I needed to focus on my daughter.

Nearly two years after the stroke, I forgave her father and went on to become pregnant with my son, Jordan. With Jordan, I was immediately met with harsh judgment. The first OBGYN in Charlotte, NC was horrible! He questioned me about how I took care of Camryn at home as if I was under interrogation for a crime and pressured me to abort my son. I went to another practice and was told that two kids was too much for me as if she had any insight into my life and support system. The only thing that allowed the tiniest bit of respect for her was her honesty in her lack of confidence in her ability to provide care due to my paralysis and stroke after I had my daughter.

She referred me to the local main hospital's high-risk gynecology and obstetrics, where I received the best care possible with an interdisciplinary team of my neurologist, urologist, and primary care physician. Even though the high-risk clinic was not accessible, I was treated with dignity and respect.

I moved to North Carolina in 2004 with my baby girl after landing my dream job as an Independent Living Specialist at the Center for Independent Living in Charlotte. I was thriving and traveling the country with my new job, then I got pregnant with my son, Jordan, in 2005. He was born prematurely with underdeveloped lungs. Similar doubts about my parenting abilities arose even more because of Jordan being born so tiny and sick. It led to a constant fear of losing custody of my children. I did allow my mom, who was a nurse, to take him for about nine months to help with him medically until he was more stable. It felt like someone had punched me in my gut the day I sent him with her.

I saw him every weekend and continued to work and was so blessed to become a homeowner through Habitat for Humanity almost a year after having my son, and he was able to come and live with me again. I left their father for good and I gained a huge support system with my neighbors who had children close in age to Camryn and Jordan. We were a village that looked out for each other throughout the years. Despite the drama with their father and harsh judgments about my decision to become a mother, I persevered with my village and have two of the most amazing kids on the planet.

Waist Deep

In 2013, I discovered Zumba and became a licensed instructor, focusing on teaching people with disabilities. I integrated Zumba into WEAN's health and fitness services and even taught classes at CMC Main's SCI inpatient hospital. Watching WEAN grow and seeing the joy Zumba brought to others was deeply fulfilling. However, at the same time, my dream job at the CIL was turning into a nightmare.

Leadership at the CIL tolerated blatant racism from a white coworker, who consistently provided poor service to Black and People of Color clients—referred to as "consumers" by the organization. I always disliked that term; it felt impersonal and dehumanizing to the very people we were supposed to serve. This coworker not only disrespected those we were helping but also stole from them and the agency. Despite numerous complaints and reports, the toxic behavior remained unchecked, leaving me increasingly disillusioned and frustrated.

The CIL's problems were compounded by poor leadership. Benefits were cut, hours were reduced, and the staff dwindled to a skeleton crew as people were either fired or left to escape the abusive work environment. Unable to find alternative employment in North Carolina, I applied for a job three hours away at a progressive and well-managed CIL in South Carolina.

I was so disheartened by my experience at the Charlotte CIL that I was ready to leave behind the support and comfort of my village. I was prepared to sell my home and commute until I could settle in South Carolina. My brother urged me to be patient, advising me not to let the hardships of my job push me away from everything I had built here. But he didn't understand the daily reality of being a disabled Black woman navigating constant microaggressions and blatant racism. I felt I had no choice but to seek a fresh start elsewhere.

On my way to the interview, I was ran off the interstate by semi-truck. I should have taken heed to that as a sign to turn around and go home. I shook it off and got back on the road. I had a lovely interview and got the job.

The following Monday, I had a one-on-one meeting with the CIL director in Charlotte. During our conversation, she informed me that my position would have to transition to part-time. The look on her face was priceless when I responded by letting her know I had already secured a part-time job with a progressive CIL in South Carolina and would be leaving.

Surprised, she asked if I might consider working with both agencies, noting all the effort I had put into establishing the women's program in Charlotte. She also suggested the possibility of a partnership for an upcoming women's conference. After some discussion, both CIL directors agreed on a joint venture, allowing me to continue my work in Charlotte on a limited basis until my new role in South Carolina transitioned to full-time.

We arranged a schedule that worked for everyone: I would work Monday through Thursday in South Carolina and dedicated Fridays to the Charlotte CIL. It was a temporary solution, giving me the opportunity to close the chapter in Charlotte while preparing for a fresh start in South Carolina.

On my first day at the new job in South Carolina, I got a flat tire on the interstate. Panic set in immediately. "I can't be late on my first day! Please, God, help me!" I pulled off at the next exit and into a Taco Bell parking lot. Thankfully, I crossed paths with two kind men who offered to put my spare tire on for me.

By some miracle, I made it on time, but as I sat there, a still small voice whispered, "Damn, Maybe Chris was right." As wonderful as the staff and agency in South Carolina were, I felt a tug in my spirit—a sense that maybe I wasn't meant to take this job after all. Something deep inside urged me to stay in North Carolina.

On December 13th, on my way to work in South Carolina, a distracted driver, who was texting, ran a stop sign and T-boned my van—the one I drove from my wheelchair. The impact was so violent that it thrust my van across the road, slamming it into a guardrail with a tree behind it. The van nearly folded like an accordion. Despite being secured by my EZ Lock system, the force bent the footplates on my power chair, twisting my feet backward and nearly amputating my right foot. My left femur and tibia were broken, along with several bones in my feet. Pain and shock consumed me as the reality hit. *Fuck! I should have listened to my brother. The ancestors were warning me! Lord, what do you want from me now?*

A man in military fatigues appeared at my side to help. I remained calm and asked him to call my mom, while the driver who hit me stood nearby, looking either stunned or high. He reassured me, saying, "Let me call 911 first, then we'll call your mom."

At the hospital, the surgeon delivered grim news: he might have to amputate my foot. My mom, standing beside me, repeated his words, making sure I understood the weight of what he was saying. "Do you understand what the doctor said?" she asked.

I responded calmly, "Yes, I do."

When I woke up from surgery, both of my feet were still intact, though encased in massive pink casts on both legs that made me feel like I weighed 600 pounds. My thoughts immediately turned to my kids, especially with Christmas just around the corner. My son was heartbroken that I wouldn't be home for the holidays.

I spent Christmas in the hospital in South Carolina, one of the hardest times of my life, second only to the nine months when Jordan stayed with my mom. My family brought the kids to visit me, but the weight of missing such a special time with them was almost unbearable.

Eventually, I was transferred back to North Carolina for therapy. After 2 ½ months in the hospital, I finally went home, but the road to recovery stretched on for four long years. I had to start over—getting a new wheelchair, receiving a new adaptive vehicle, and figuring out what life looked like now.

I couldn't return to my job in South Carolina, and I made the decision to quit the CIL in Charlotte. The director, who had been notably absent during my hospitalization, tried to take WEAN from me, the very program I had built. She was the only one from the CIL who didn't call or visit, but my coworkers kept me informed of every move she made to undermine my work.

With the help of Janice, WEAN's founder, and the support of my coworkers, we stopped her. WEAN remained mine, and as soon as I was able, I turned my focus to figuring out how to move forward into my purpose.

Swimming in the Deep

Despite the challenges, injuries, mistreatment, and disrespect I faced, I refused to let adversity define me. Instead, I poured my energy into helping others, teaching Zumba for the next eight years, and acquiring new skills in SEO writing and digital marketing. After enduring multiple medical traumas and life dramas, some might have thought, *"Sis, you need to stop. Give up."* But my response was different. I believed my purpose must be mighty because, after facing death three times, it was clear that something was working overtime to take me out.

It was after the second car accident in 2013 that I truly understood my purpose and how I had been working through such challenges. I reflected on four extraordinary women I had mentored over the years—Asha, Mia, Miriam, and Raven. I call them my *Wheel Sisters.*

My job was far more demanding than typical case management. It required me to be open, vulnerable, and share the deepest, rawest parts of my life as a Black woman and mom living with a disability. Together, my Wheel Sisters and I have navigated the trenches and celebrated the triumphs of being Black, female, and disabled—experiences that many will never fully understand.

After that accident, these women loved on me fiercely. They reminded me of how my work, love, time, and energy had profoundly impacted their lives. Their unwavering support and the bonds we shared made me realize that my purpose was more than mighty—it was *divine.* I remained obedient to the call on my life, focusing on my *why* and living fully. God continued to bless me with even more Wheel Sisters, more women to love and lean on, and more stories to celebrate.

Today, I proudly share the stories of these incredible women in North Carolina as an Ambassador for *The Raw Beauty Project*, a visual art exhibit. Telling these stories and celebrating the trials and victories of my Wheel

Sisters has empowered me and countless others beyond measure. Each story is a testament to resilience, community, and divine purpose.

Floating in My Glory

Living in your purpose and doing the work can sometimes feel overwhelming. It can pull you into deep, uncertain waters, where the currents are strong and staying afloat requires everything you've got. But in those moments, remember this: don't panic. Instead, lean into the flow. Relax, trust, and let the water work for you.

I encourage everyone to never give up—but just as importantly, to take time to rest. Rest is not a sign of weakness; it's a necessary pause to recharge before weariness takes over. Step back, catch your breath, and then return to your path with renewed energy and focus.

Live life like a mermaid. Swim fearlessly into the deep, venture into the unknown, and trust in the strength that carries you. Move boldly and confidently in your divine purpose, knowing that even in uncharted waters, you are equipped to navigate.

Through every challenge, I've embraced life in all its depths—its joys, pains, and triumphs. Like the sea, my journey has been vast, unpredictable, and profoundly beautiful, shaped by resilience, faith, and self-discovery. I am a mermaid, unafraid of the deep, forever swimming toward my purpose with grace, courage, and intention.

About the Author

Monique Stamps is a trailblazer whose life took a remarkable turn after a devastating car accident at the age of 16 left her paralyzed from the chest down. Despite this life-altering event, she transformed adversity into opportunity, earning a Bachelor's degree in Social Work and dedicating over 20 years to advocating for disability rights.

In Charlotte, NC, Monique established a sister chapter of Women Embracing Abilities Now (W.E.A.N.), fostering peer mentoring relationships for women and girls with disabilities. Through this initiative, she champions equal access to breast and OB/GYN care and raises awareness of the significant health disparities faced by individuals with disabilities.

Monique champions sisterhood among women with disabilities, amplifying their voices and challenging stereotypes. As Outreach Coordinator for The Raw Beauty Project, she expands its impact, advocating for inclusion and equality..

Monique's dedication extends to her role as an ambassador for *The Raw Beauty Project*, where she curated a 2016 exhibit spotlighting models and photographers from the Charlotte area. Her efforts have expanded the project's reach, bringing its empowering message to other cities in North Carolina. Now serving as the Outreach Coordinator for *The Raw Beauty Project* and its health initiatives, Monique continues to inspire and advocate for inclusion and equality.

How to Connect with Monique:

Email: m.stamps@weanqc.com
Instagram: @moniquestamps522
LinKedIn: Monique Stamps

Acknowledgements

This work is dedicated to my beautiful children, Camryn and Jordan, who are my heart and my inspiration. To my mother, Ruth, my sister, Ginna, and my brother, Chris, for their endless love and support. Rest in peace, Dad, Gary; your memory lives on in everything I do. To my sisters by love, LeEtta and Kendra Hart, Maria Pahang, and Mindy Stewart, whose strength and friendship have been pillars in my life. To my wheel sisters, Twila Adams, Keisha Belchee, Asha Toure, Mia Jenkins, Miriam Penn, Raven Robinson (RIP), Gentle Mitchell, Talathia McKenzie Jr., Ashley Tatum, Xuan Truong, and Kebra Moore, who have shared in the triumphs and struggles of our journeys together.

To my caregiver and comfort, Edgitha Jnbaptiste, whose care and kindness have been unwavering. To my favorite accomplices, Jules Springs, Carolyn Covington, Debbie Myers, Wendy Crawford, and Susan Solman, for always being by my side. Finally, to my guiding angels Grandma Jeanette and Grandaddy David, Aunt Carolyn, and Aunt Puddin, whose spirits continue to guide and watch over me. Your love, strength, and support have shaped my journey, and I am forever grateful.

Kebra C. Moore, Visionary Author

Author, Singer, Song Writer
Ms. Wheelchair Mississippi 2013
Founder, Welcome To The Storm Publishing!
Founder, Tropical Storm Collection

The Tree That Saved my Life!

A Road Trip: The Night Everything Changed

In 1999, I was living in New Orleans, LA, and for the first time, I felt like I was truly beginning to build the life I'd always dreamed of. I was a graduate student at the University of New Orleans, working towards my master's degree in music education, a path that I was passionate about. With my 13 months old son, and my role as a music teacher in an elementary school, life felt full. On top of it all, I was engaged to the love of my life. It felt like everything was aligning perfectly.

As a college graduate from Claflin University, where I also majored in Music Education, I knew the value of hard work and perseverance. I'd been raised by my mother, who instilled in me the importance of resilience, and later, during my sophomore year of high school, I moved in with my aunt and uncle. They provided even more support and guidance, helping me stay focused on my goals.

Christmas Eve that year was filled with excitement. My fiancé and I decided to take a road trip from New Orleans to Camden, Arkansas, to celebrate the holidays with his brother. We packed up the SUV, filling it with gifts for our son, and made sure to return the video we'd rented – it was the era of video rentals, after all. With everything in place, we hit the road, the car packed with holiday spirit and excitement for what lay ahead.

But life has a way of changing in an instant. About two hours into our drive, as we passed through Utica, Mississippi, something unimaginable happened. A series of events that I never could have anticipated led to a moment that would change my life forever. My name is Kebra Chenise Harris-Moore, and I have a spinal cord injury.

Spinal cord injuries (SCIs) are complex and vary widely in severity and impact. Some people, after such an injury, experience paralysis, while others may have reduced mobility or chronic pain. Spinal cord injuries are generally classified by the level and completeness of the injury. When the spinal cord is injured, it disrupts the communication between the brain and the body. In my case, it affected my ability to walk and move freely.

There are different types of spinal cord injuries, from complete to incomplete injuries, depending on whether any nerve pathways are left intact. In a complete spinal cord injury, all feeling and movement below the injury level are lost, but in an incomplete injury, some function remains. Each person's journey and experience with SCI is unique, and the physical, emotional, and psychological effects can be profound. The injury itself is life-altering, but so are the daily realities, the adjustments, and the perseverance it requires.

It was a small mistake, just an accidental slip by an elderly driver, but it changed everything in an instant. Our vehicle suddenly inclined and crashed into a tree. In many ways, that tree saved my life, along with the lives of my fiancé and our small child. I'll never forget the terrifying moment of hearing his cries from the back seat, realizing I couldn't move, and feeling this overwhelming sense of helplessness. Thankfully, he was unharmed but shaken. My fiancé then asked me if I was okay, and that's when I understood—I couldn't move. Pain shot through my back, and fear overwhelmed me.

Behind us, a crowd had started to gather, and several people were already calling 911. Amidst the chaos, I heard the sound of sirens approaching. But one woman, *an angel* as I now call her, stood out. She was the driver in the car right behind us, an emergency room nurse who stepped in to help immediately. She leaned in and told me not to move, her calm and compassionate voice steadying my panic. She asked if I believed in God and if she could pray for me. In that moment, her prayer became my strength, something to hold onto while we waited for the ambulance to arrive.

When the paramedics arrived, they moved quickly, trying to get me out of the car as safely as possible. They took us to Utica Hospital, where the reality of my injuries began to sink in. I remember them cutting my bra off to do the X-rays, a small detail that felt strangely significant in that moment. I heard my son crying in a room nearby, and all I could think about was him, worrying if he was truly okay. The doctors and nurses assured me that he and my fiancé were both fine, and as much as I wanted to see them, they insisted they had to focus on me first. The results of the X-ray soon confirmed what they suspected: I had sustained a spinal cord injury at the T12 level.

The *T12 level* refers to the twelfth thoracic vertebra, which is near the lower part of the spine, just above the lumbar region. The thoracic spine supports the ribs and chest, helping protect vital organs. Damage to the spinal cord at this level affects muscles and sensation from the waist down. Because my injury was at the T12 level, it disrupted signals to and from the lower part of my body, resulting in a significant loss of sensation and movement.

Spinal cord injuries vary widely in severity and impact. Some people with T12 injuries may retain partial mobility and sensation, while others may experience complete paralysis below the injury. My injury was serious, altering the course of my life in unimaginable ways. Every day since then has been a journey of learning, adapting, and finding new ways to live fully despite the limitations.

Because Utica Hospital didn't have the specialized technology needed to treat a spinal cord injury (SCI), the doctors arranged to transfer me to St. Dominic Memorial Hospital in Jackson, Mississippi. My fiancé had to make one of the hardest calls of his life: he phoned my family to tell them what happened. As soon as my mom heard, she dropped everything and caught the first flight to Mississippi. By the time she arrived, the swelling in my spine was severe, and I had to wear a heavy back brace. The pain was constant, unlike anything I'd ever felt, but having my family by my side helped me hold on.

January 4, 2000

January 2, 2000, was the day that everything changed. The doctors informed me I needed surgery. The spinal swelling wasn't going down, and the damage at my T12 level was serious. Surgery was necessary to stabilize my spine and prevent further damage. On January 4, 2000, I was terrified but ready; I knew this was the only chance for me to have any hope of recovery. The surgery was extensive, involving nerve repair and thoracic fusion. They fused my spine from T11 to T12, effectively binding the vertebrae together to stabilize my back.

After surgery, I was transferred to the ICU. My mom was right by my side, a comforting presence in the middle of all the chaos. I had never experienced drugs like these before, and they sent my mind to a place I could hardly recognize. I wasn't myself. The pain was raw and intense, and I was lashing out at everyone, my mom, the nurses, even the doctors. I remember cursing them out, words spilling out in frustration and agony, until finally, they had to give me something to calm me down.

The pain was a constant, throbbing reminder of the trauma my body had been through, unlike anything I'd ever known. Tubes hung out from my body to monitor blood flow and prevent infections. The nurses were clear that spinal cord injuries often come with severe risks of blood clots, so every 12 hours, they injected me with blood thinners.

Yet, in those moments, I found strength I never knew I had. God, in His wisdom, knew better, giving me the resilience to face that pain and all that lay ahead. Each heartbeat and every breath felt like a struggle, but I kept holding on, leaning on my faith, on my family, and on the love that surrounded me.

My fiancé never left my side. He had orders to be stationed in California, but he couldn't imagine leaving me and our son here alone, so we made a decision that would surprise everyone. He came to me one night, his eyes filled with love and determination, and said, "Let's move the wedding date up. I want us to be married."

There was a small courthouse right next to the hospital, and after he spoke to the judge, he decided that on January 6, he would come to my bedside, and we would get married right there in the hospital. The nurses and hospital staff, who had all become like family in those days, were nothing short of amazing. They washed my hair, helped style it, and even brought in a bit of makeup to make me feel beautiful for this unexpected ceremony.

On the morning of January 6, he came in, ready to make good on his promise to love and protect me through anything. The judge arrived, and from my hospital bed, I became Mrs. Marquis Moore. It wasn't the wedding we'd planned, but it was something *deeper*, something *real*. Marquis proved that he loved me not just in the best of times but in the hardest moments of our lives. It's a memory that will always remind me of his unwavering strength and commitment.

The hospital staff celebrated with us, filling the room with as much joy and laughter as they could. Even though I was far from healed and still faced an uncertain road ahead, that day reminded me I wasn't in this fight alone. Marquis and I had each other, and together, we could take on anything.

The Wind Beneath Me

It had been about two weeks since my transfer to St. Dominic's, where every day brought a new layer of reality, I wasn't ready to face. Physical therapy had started, but each session was a reminder of the journey ahead. Then one morning, a woman walked into my room. She looked to be in her mid-thirties, a Caucasian woman in scrubs, with a kind, gentle face. Her demeanor was soft, but there was *confidence* in her step, as if she had done this countless times before. I didn't know who she was, but she introduced herself as my therapist.

The word "therapist" barely registered with me. I had never, in all my life, seen one, and I wasn't sure what she was here to do for me now. But she was polite, and she spoke with a careful sensitivity to my pain, her voice soothing and steady. She sat by my bed and leaned in, her eyes sincere, telling me that she "understood" what I was going through. I wanted to believe her. But with each visit, my frustration grew.

On her third visit, I couldn't hold it in anymore. "What do you understand?" I asked, my voice heavy with disbelief. "How can you come in here day by day telling me you understand? You walk in here, whole, and healthy. How can you understand this?" I gestured to my body, now confined to a bed, struggling to adjust to a new reality. My anger spilled out like I'd been holding it back for years. I didn't want to see her, didn't want to hear her words. She looked at me, silent, and nodded as if my words were something she expected. She didn't argue or defend herself, just gave me space to release what I was holding inside. But when she left, that anger stayed with me, lingering long after she was gone.

That night, I couldn't hold back my emotions any longer. Alone in my hospital room, I cried out to God. "Why?" I asked, my voice hoarse, barely more than a whisper. "Why am I going through this?" I thought of my sins, my mistakes, my regrets. Was this God's way of punishing me? Was I paying for every wrong choice, every moment I wished I could take back?

The tears streamed down my face, deep tears of despair that I could feel in my chest. I looked over at the window, its curtains swaying softly, as the cool night air brought a strange comfort. The medication they had given me was wearing off, and I felt myself shifting from cold to hot in waves.

In that vulnerable moment, I made a plea. "God, if I'm going to be okay, if there's some purpose in this, please… please, show me. Just let me feel it." The words were barely out when I felt a gust of wind blow through the room, so strong that the curtains whipped back and forth, filling the room with a sense of something greater than myself. I felt *His presence*, a warmth that surrounded me in the middle of my pain. He was telling me I was going to be okay. In that instant, I knew that He was with me, guiding me, promising that even in this dark valley, He was by my side.

I lay back on the bed, a deep calm settling over me. I didn't have all the answers, but I had something I hadn't felt in weeks—a glimmer of hope. The road ahead would be long, and I knew I would have to learn to live in a wheelchair, to adapt to a body that no longer moved the way it once had. But I also knew I wasn't alone.

I had a family that needed me—a new husband, a son to raise. And I had *faith*, rekindled in the stillness of that night, reminding me that even now, my life had purpose. I was ready to face the unknown, ready to learn what it would take to build this new life. I wasn't just a patient or a victim. I was a mother, a wife, and, above all, a child of God, chosen to walk a path that He was lighting before me.

The journey wouldn't be easy. But for the first time since the accident, I felt ready to face it.

Breaking and Rebuilding Faith

After a month at St. Dominic's, it was finally time to take the next step—a step that would force me to confront my new reality. I was being transferred to Touro Rehabilitation Center in New Orleans, LA. The work of healing and rebuilding would begin. This next phase felt both promising and terrifying, a necessary journey that would evaluate everything I believed in.

At Touro, I met Dr. Hammerly, my physiatrist. A *physiatrist* specializes in physical medicine and rehabilitation, helping people recover from serious injuries and regain as much function as possible. Dr. Hammerly was warm and kind, patiently answering my questions. My biggest question was about the status of my injury, was it complete or incomplete? That single detail would make all the difference.

After a thorough examination, he told me I had an incomplete spinal cord injury. Relief washed over me. An incomplete injury meant there was a chance, however slim, that I could regain some movement over time. I already had some movement in my left leg and a limited amount in my right. It was a small sign, but it gave me hope—a glimmer that God wasn't finished with me yet.

With that hope came determination. I thought of my husband and son, who came to visit me every single day, their presence a constant reminder of my purpose. Seeing them filled me with a joy that kept me going, even when the days felt long and the therapy difficult. My extended family visited when they could, but they had lives to return to. Marquis and MJ, though, were my anchors. They were my strength, and I knew I had to keep pushing forward for them.

Then, one day, I got a phone call that shook me to my core. It was from an old college friend, someone who had been like family to me. Hearing her voice filled me with happiness at first, as if life before the accident was close enough to touch. She said she wanted to pray for me, and I welcomed it. But as her prayer ended, she told me something that felt like a knife to my heart: she believed I was in this wheelchair because God was punishing me.

In an instant, all the faith I'd worked to rebuild, all the hope I'd clung to, felt shattered. Her words lingered, casting shadows over every bit of peace I'd managed to hold onto. How could she say that? How could she think that a loving God would punish me in such a way? I was left feeling lost and hurt, with my faith bruised and fragile all over again. Her words stayed with me, gnawing at my spirit.

I called a family member, my voice shaking as I shared what my friend had said. She listened quietly, then firmly reminded me, "God doesn't punish His children like this. He loves you, and He will heal you in His time." Her voice was gentle yet strong, a balm over my wounds. She prayed with me right there on the phone, reminding me of God's promise in Jeremiah 30:17: ***"For I will restore health to you and heal you of your wounds,"*** says the Lord. Those words touched me deeply, and I felt a bit of peace returning, as if God were once again drawing close.

After we ended the call, I reflected on my journey, on how faith isn't always steady and unbreakable. Sometimes, it shatters, and we have to pick up the pieces and rebuild them over and over again. I realized then that this journey wasn't just about healing my body; it was about restoring my faith, about learning to trust in a God who had never abandoned me.

Rising Against all Odds

Five months in the hospital felt like a lifetime, each day blending into the next as I learned to live in a completely new way. I had to start from scratch, figuring out how to cook, bathe, transfer, and simply exist in this new reality from my wheelchair. Occupational therapy was grueling. Every task that used to come so easily was now a mountain to climb. But one of the hardest parts was having Marquis there, seeing me struggle. I wanted to be strong for him, for MJ, for myself—but some days, the strength just wasn't there.

It wasn't just the physical challenges that weighed on me. I heard the whispers, the disrespectful comments from some of the CNAs who claimed Marquis wouldn't stay, that he'd eventually leave because I couldn't walk. They looked at me with pity, assuming my life was over, that my marriage couldn't survive this. I had to endure their negativity, pushing through the judgment and naysayers to learn what I could and create a new life. I clung to my faith and reminded myself of Philippians 4:13: *"I can do all things through Christ who strengthens me."*

Eight months later, my family gathered in my hospital room for a meeting. It was time—I was finally being discharged from inpatient therapy and would start outpatient therapy from home. This was another huge step, and it was overwhelming. I knew I'd have to adapt everything I'd learned in therapy to my life at home, where I'd be a wife, mother, and homemaker again. Balancing therapy every day with running a household and Marquis working half days was tough. Financially, it was a struggle, but somehow, by God's grace, we made it work. Little by little, I started to feel a glimmer of confidence returning.

After a year of outpatient therapy, my body grew stronger, and my heart grew more determined. One day, I rolled into a mall for a rare bit of shopping, something I hadn't done in so long. As I passed a full-length mirror, I saw myself, fully, in my wheelchair, and it broke me. I stared at my reflection, the reality of my new life staring back. All the emotions I'd pushed down came flooding out. Tears filled my eyes, and a wave of sadness and despair washed over me. I felt so different, so far from the woman I used to be. Depression hit hard, and for a moment, I wanted to turn away.

But then, something shifted. I wiped my tears, looked at myself, and thought, *Kebra, this is your reality. You're still here, still alive, still blessed with your family. The world isn't stopping for you—you have to decide if you're going to keep going.* And in that moment, I chose to keep going, to keep fighting, to live my life fully.

Then came the biggest change of all—we were moving to San Diego. Marquis, MJ, and I were starting fresh, and while I was excited about the new beginning, I was equally terrified. San Diego was a big, bustling city, and I didn't know a soul there. For the first time, I'd be managing my family without the comfort of familiar support nearby. I had no choice but to dig deep and find my inner strength, to adapt to this new chapter, and to be the best wife and mother I could be from my wheelchair.

Before the move, I went to Georgia while Marquis was searching for a place for us in San Diego. During that trip, I stayed with a close family member, but things didn't go as planned. We ended up having one of the biggest disagreements that we'd ever had. It was hard for her to see me in the wheelchair, and her frustration came to the surface when my 2-year-old started acting defiant. She was overwhelmed, and I could feel her pain in the way she spoke. Her frustration wasn't just about the moment, it was about the weight of everything we were all dealing with.

My new reality was hard on all of us. We were all hurting in different ways, trying to navigate this unfamiliar terrain and find a new normal. It wasn't just my life that had changed; it affected everyone around me. Despite the disagreement, I knew her frustration stemmed from love and concern, and even though it stung in the moment, it was part of the journey we were all on—learning how to adjust, how to heal, and how to support each other through the challenges.

Within a year of my accident, I got the unexpected news—I was pregnant. Fear gripped me as I tried to imagine being pregnant and parenting from a wheelchair. How would I do this? Could my body manage the strain? When I visited my OB-GYN, I was immediately classified as a high-risk pregnancy. I was afraid, but the pregnancy went better than I'd dared to hope. No morning sickness, no complications, just pure, miraculous growth of new life.

And as my belly grew, I wanted something more—I wanted a wedding. Even though Marquis and I were already married, I dreamed of walking down the aisle. Therapy became my battleground as I learned to walk with braces. I pushed myself harder than I ever had, all for that moment when I'd be able to walk to Marquis.

On January 6, 2001, our first anniversary, that dream came true. Family came from all over to witness our vows, and my heart swelled with gratitude. My Uncle Tony helped steady me, allowing me to walk down the aisle with my walker and braces, and when I reached Marquis, I felt more victorious than ever before. I was three months pregnant, standing tall with my man, hand in hand, knowing that nothing could break us.

Unfortunately, our son was born prematurely at 32 weeks, arriving breech. It was a tense, uncertain time, but he made it through, and we brought him home, healthy and strong. Now, I was a mother of two beautiful boys, with a toddler and a newborn, learning to balance my new role as a wife, mother, and woman in a wheelchair.

Life was harder than I'd ever imagined. The car became both a lifeline and a challenge—a space where I had to carefully coordinate two car seats and my wheelchair. Loading and unloading my wheelchair while ensuring both boys were secure was a feat that required patience, creativity, and determination. Every trip was a test of endurance, whether it was a doctor's appointment, a grocery run or simply trying to give my boys the joy of a day at the park.

Through God's grace, I managed. Each day, I discovered new ways to adapt, from figuring out how to get my chair into the car with one hand while holding my newborn in the other, to mastering the art of buckling my toddler in while still keeping a watchful eye on my baby. I didn't know how I'd do it all, but each day I found strength, and each day I was reminded of the blessings in my life.

There were moments of exhaustion and tears, but they were outweighed by the laughter of my toddler as he discovered the world and the peaceful coos of my newborn in my arms. Being a mother in a wheelchair taught me resilience like nothing else. It taught me to appreciate the smallest victories and to lean into the profound love I had for my family. I wasn't just surviving—I was *thriving*, one small triumph at a time.

This journey, with all its trials, joys, and triumphs, became my testament to faith, resilience, and the grace of God. The journey was far from over, but with every step, I became stronger, and I knew that, somehow, I would make it.

I didn't know what the future held or if my body would fully recover, but I understood that **_faith is tested most in times of darkness._** Even when it wavered, I would keep choosing to believe in God's plan for me. With the love of my family, the support of those who truly cared, and a God who would walk with me through every step of this journey, I knew I could find strength, one day at a time.

The Journey Continues

Through the years, challenges came and went like the tides—some washing away my strength, others bringing new opportunities. I lost friends and gained new ones, but one thing remained constant: my love and commitment to my sorority, Delta Sigma Theta Sorority, Inc. My boys grew, and my marriage evolved through its ups and downs, but God kept us steady and my boys safe. There were moments when people talked about me, laughed at me, and said some of the most disrespectful things that triggered painful memories of my injury. Those moments stung deeply, cutting into my sense of self-worth and challenging my ability to move forward. Recently, I experienced hurtful actions and words from individuals who were supposed to share a sisterly bond with me. It was a painful reminder that no matter how much love you think you've given or how genuine your intentions are, people will often show you how they truly feel in their actions and words.

These challenges, though deeply hurtful, have been some of my greatest teachers. They have taught me resilience in the face of adversity and the importance of maintaining grace and kindness even when others fail to do the same. I've learned that my worth is not defined by the opinions or actions of others but by the love and purpose God has placed within me. I've discovered the power of maturity, understanding that responding to negativity with anger or bitterness only allows it to fester. Instead, I've chosen to rise above, to protect my peace, and to focus on my growth.

Returning to therapy was a decision that came from a deep need to address the emotional and psychological scars that I had carried for so long. I was finally ready to confront the trauma I'd been holding onto. Molested by a family member during my childhood, left a wound that never truly healed, a weight I carried silently as life went on. Later, as a single parent during the times my husband was deployed, I faced the strain of raising a family alone, with all its challenges and loneliness. And then there was the injury, which felt like one more burden on top of an already heavy load.

It was a time when I could have really used support, but instead, I found myself battling hurtful rumors started by another military spouse, making me feel isolated from the very community that should have been my refuge. That betrayal cut deep, as it came at a time when I was most vulnerable. Through each of these experiences, the pain and the weight seemed to only grow, settling beneath the surface of my daily life.

But as I dug deeper in therapy, I began to see that God had already planted within me the strength to endure. What I needed now was *the courage* to allow that strength to heal me—not just physically, but in my heart and mind as well. I learned that healing goes beyond restoring the body; it means nurturing the spirit and reclaiming peace within myself. Stepping into this journey hasn't been easy, but I know it's essential for my wholeness. And with faith as my anchor, I'm finding that I am stronger than I ever realized. This journey is about reclaiming my life, one day, one step at a time.

Today, I stand proud as a business owner with my own lipstick line, a singer, a songwriter, and the author of five bestselling novels. I run my own publishing company, a dream I once thought was out of reach. My Amazon bestseller, *Love, Lies, & Music,* is being adapted into a TV mini-series, bringing my story to a new audience and expanding its reach. My boys are now adults—one is in graduate school and an alumnus of Claflin University, while the other proudly served as a military veteran. They are my greatest achievements, constant reminders of resilience and strength, and they inspire me every day.

I still attend physical therapy now and then to maintain my strength. With the support of one brace and my walker, I'm able to stand and walk. I drive independently, travel, cook, and clean—and, after all these years, Marquis and I are still happily married. Life hasn't always been easy, but God has kept me grounded with a steady mind and a grateful heart.

One of the most unexpected honors was having my song, "He'll Make a Way," featured in the documentary *Becoming Barack,* about President Barack Obama. And being crowned Ms. Wheelchair Mississippi, 2013 was a true highlight; it gave me the opportunity to advocate for accessibility, and I worked tirelessly to help make some state facilities handicap accessible.

Even at the military bases where we were stationed, I lobbied for improvements, advocating for accessibility that had previously been overlooked. My voice became a beacon of change, and I am proud to have contributed to making spaces more inclusive.

I am strong, resilient, and unstoppable. I have learned that life is a precious gift. I love God, my family, and more importantly, I cherish life itself. I have faced the depths of despair and emerged with a greater understanding of my purpose. My journey has taught me that strength comes in many forms, and through faith, hard work, and love, anything is possible.

As I close this chapter of my life and reflect on my journey, I am filled with hope and gratitude. I know that the path ahead may still hold challenges, but with God as my guide, I will continue to rise. I am ready for whatever comes next, fully embracing my journey and the beautiful life I've been blessed to live.

Thank you for walking this journey with me. May you find strength and hope in your own paths, and may you always remember that no matter the obstacles, you, too, can rise.

About the Author

Kebra C. Moore, a dynamic and inspirational figure, hails from Beaufort, South Carolina, and now resides in Texas. A proud graduate of Claflin University in Orangeburg, South Carolina, with a degree in Music Education, Kebra has dedicated her life to blending her artistic talents with advocacy and education. She is the owner of *Welcome To The Storm Publishing* and *Tropical Storm Collection* lip line.

Kebra's passion for music has been a lifelong journey. A gifted singer and songwriter, her number-one song, *He'll Make a Way*, was prominently featured in the documentary *Becoming Barack*, chronicling the life of President Barack Obama. Her work resonates deeply with audiences, combining soulful melodies with powerful messages of hope and resilience.

In 2013, Kebra earned the title of Ms. Wheelchair Mississippi, using her platform to make a significant impact. She advocated for and successfully led initiatives to improve accessibility throughout the state and on military bases, ensuring that individuals with disabilities could navigate these spaces with dignity and ease. Her efforts have left a lasting legacy, benefiting countless lives.

Kebra has been married to her husband, a proud military veteran, for 25 years and is the devoted mother of two sons. She is an active member of Delta Sigma Theta Sorority, Incorporated, a philanthropist, and a social activist committed to fostering positive change.

How to Connect with Kebra:

https://w2tspublishing.org/
Email: info@midnightstorm.net
FB: @Midnight Storm
Instagram: @iammidnightstormm
LinKedIn: Kebra Moore

Acknowledgements

This anthology has been a joyous journey, and I am deeply grateful to everyone who has supported me from the beginning. Your encouragement has been instrumental in shaping who I am today, and I owe much of my growth and success to your belief in me. Through it all, God has guided me, showing me what truly matters and granting me a sense of peace. I am thankful for all God's blessings and truly would not be who I am without him.

A special thank you to my other half, Marquis, for always believing in me and standing by my side. Your love, support, invaluable advice, and constant encouragement have been the foundation of my strength. I truly love you and am so blessed to have you by my side.

To my boys, thank you for growing into the incredible men you are. Your presence, love, and growth inspire me daily and mean the world to me.

To my mom and my beautiful Dunbar family, who are spread out all over, your love and support have been the foundation of my journey and my strength. I carry you in my heart with every step I take, and I am forever grateful for you all.

To my incredible team: a heartfelt thank you to my editor, Veronica "Red Diamond" Miller, for refining this anthology with such precision and care; your dedication to this project has made all the difference. To my beta reader, Shalonda "Shay" Cravins, your insightful feedback has been invaluable in shaping this work. Your contributions mean more to me than words can express.

And most importantly, to all the beautiful ladies who have contributed to this anthology—your stories, voices, and courage have elevated this project to new heights. I am deeply grateful for your hard work, vulnerability, and dedication. Together, we have created something extraordinary, and I am so proud of each of you. Let's continue to rise, inspire, and empower one another as we journey forward.

This anthology is a celebration of perseverance, creativity, and community, and it is an honor to share it with the world. Thank you to everyone who has played a part in this incredible experience. This is only the beginning—let's continue to dream, create, and uplift together.

Nelita Manego-Ramey, Contributing Author

Disability advocate, Registered Nurse
Wheelchair athlete

Mommy, You Didn't Die?

I'm going to tell you a story about my injury—the day it happened, the weeks and months of rehab that followed, the countless challenges, the endless frustrations, the bottomless aggravations, and all the disappointments that came with it. It wasn't a good time in my life. Everything was dark and uncertain, and I spent every day trying to figure out what the hell was going on.

I woke up on a hard hospital bed. The curtain was closed. Doctors were shouting orders, and phones were ringing nonstop. I was tangled in wires connected to various monitors, while an incessantly beeping pump pushed IV fluids into my veins. My legs were completely numb. It was 5:00 p.m., and the local news was playing on the TV. When I turned my head to watch, I saw, on the old staticky screen, the front of my apartment building. Two police officers were scouring the scene, and a blue high-heeled pump, knocked on its side, caught my eye. I recognized it immediately as mine. I was witnessing my story unfold in real time, and at that moment, I knew my life had been changed forever.

Go back farther? Oh, okay.

I always thought I had a pretty good childhood, all things considered.

I grew up in the 1960s, and everyone on my block was like one big family. Thinking back, all I ever knew was Catholicism. My mom would drag us to church when I didn't want to go and made sure we followed all the Catholic traditions. Education was also a priority in our house. My mother, an educator, worked tirelessly to give my sister and me the best life possible. We had everything we needed and wanted.

What we didn't have was a home without my parents arguing. Even when I was in the back of the house, hiding in my room, I could hear their loud voices. There was nothing I could do except wish it would all go away. I never talked to anyone about it because I thought everyone went through the same things in their families.

The arguing continued throughout high school. Finally, through some divine mercy, my parents divorced during my senior year. I felt relieved, but I wasn't going to stay in that home for college. Too much had already happened, and I needed to leave.

My mom and sister dropped me off at LSU on move-in day in the fall of 1979. I was excited to be on campus, far away from New Orleans, but also nervous about being on my own. Despite the jitters, I was overwhelmingly overjoyed to be free from the chaos at home.

By some strange luck, my roommate and I were staying right next to the athlete's dorm, so as soon as we finished setting up our dorm room, we headed to our downstairs lobby. It was absolutely filled to the brim with students and athletes—some walking, others talking, and the rest playing backgammon.

One of our friends who was there on a football scholarship brought us over to meet some of *his* athlete friends. I was introduced to a guy from Monroe, LA. He was handsome, *and* he was a football player, which made him even more attractive, at least to me. We talked, laughed, and before the evening was over, we exchanged numbers. I was a little giddy and excited but wasn't looking for a boyfriend.

Over the next few days, I found myself thinking about him. Pretty soon, I was starting to really like him. Crazy, right? I had butterflies in my stomach every time we saw each other. By the time Homecoming came around, I was officially his girlfriend. I never had a boyfriend before, so this was a new experience for me, and something I had never felt before. I introduced him to my mom, and *immediately*, she let me know he was *not* the one. She had said something along the lines of, "he is not your kind," but I ignored her opinion and continued to date him.

He treated me well. He opened doors for me, accompanied me to the show, and took me out to eat. He really didn't have a lot of freedom between practices, games, and that ridiculous curfew, but I was okay with that.

Before I knew it, three years had already passed, and there were so many troubled times between us. There was infidelity on his part, which really hurt me, but I took him back anyway. I guess I didn't know any better.

I grew more and more exhausted and sick of his non-caring attitude. I didn't see him in my future, so I ended things during our last year of college. It was a mutual decision.

After graduation, I moved back home to enroll in nursing school. I was free, single, and embracing a fresh start, but I still felt I was moving backwards in life.

I had to keep moving.

The local cable company was hiring customer service representatives, and this position allowed me to work without interfering too much with my nursing school curriculum. It wasn't just studying all the time, however. The local club scene and the Louisiana World's Fair in 1984 were my favorite places to hang out with my friends and classmates.

There were lots of Fridays and Saturdays in the club. It was one of those club nights that I saw him in the crowd. I was shocked. I thought about how he treated me and how miserable I was when we were together. But I guess that didn't matter to me much. We danced and talked as if nothing ever happened. As the night ended, he said that he'd call me soon. I was flattered but didn't hold on to his words.

He did indeed call. And he kept calling. Calling, calling, calling. Over and over and over. Believe me, I was excited that he wanted to be with me, but I wasn't completely sure if I wanted to be with him. My friends reminded me of the past, but I didn't listen. I wanted to give him another chance.

We met with friends and went out to dinner. Weeks and months passed, and I spent more and more time with him. Every glance and touch was exhilarating. As time went on, we grew more inseparable. We couldn't see each other with anyone else.

We often talked about our goals and dreams for the future. He had been working odd jobs and was seeking steady employment. After months of looking, he was moving to San Antonio to accept a job with the Sheriff's Office. For me, this news came at the worse time. I cried and wondered why. Why now? He assured me that the distance would not affect our relationship nor how he felt about me. We stayed connected and he visited often.

He popped the question to me on New Year's Eve, 1985, in his hometown of Monroe. I said *yes*, even though there were some family and friends of mine who wished I had said *no*. We planned to wed the following year.

My dream came true on November 22, 1986. Our wedding was perfect, surrounded by loved ones. It was the happiest day of my life. After a honeymoon in Orlando, Florida, we moved to San Antonio. I had already accepted a job as a staff nurse at the county hospital.

I wanted to be the best wife. I cooked his favorite meals, washed his clothes, and always cleaned up after him. I loved this man so much. He made me feel safe and secure. He was my knight in shining armor.

Of course, we disagreed on some issues, but it wasn't anything we couldn't resolve. Most of the disagreements were about our finances. He contributed somewhat to household expenses, but I was the breadwinner and paid most of the bills. This began to weigh heavily on me, so I worked extra shifts at a hospital near the Texas/Mexico border. I didn't want bad credit, so I did what I had to do.

He decided to switch to the daytime shift. Now I was really getting mad. He knew I wouldn't see him as much because I was still on the nighttime shift. Over the course of a few months, he wouldn't come home after work. I suspected infidelity, but he denied it.

Pretty soon, our marriage was inundated with arguments about core values and broken trust. He berated me with insults and personal attacks. It felt like the marriage was nearing its end, but I didn't want that to happen. It couldn't.

In 1990, an opportunity came for me to move back to Baton Rouge and start a new job. That was perfect since I was already missing home. I was so burned out from working nights in the NICU, and overall, just tired of trying to keep this marriage going.

A few months after moving to Baton Rouge, my mom was diagnosed with cancer. She began an aggressive treatment plan. As a nurse, I was aware of the expected outcomes and complications. As a daughter, I was *devastated*. My full attention had shifted from salvaging my marriage to taking care of my mother.

My mother's cancer spread to other parts of her body. I had been begging her to stop working, and she eventually agreed. She decided to try one last aggressive chemotherapy drug. It was not successful, so hospice care was offered. She declined. My sister and I hired sitters for evenings and nights and my grandmother sat with her during the day.

I commuted from Baton Rouge to New Orleans to run errands, pay bills, and spend quality time with her. I knew her days were numbered. We would reminisce about the past and talk about the future. One topic I did not discuss was my marriage. She did not need to worry about me.

My mom succumbed to cancer on August 10, 1990. It was the saddest day of my life. My rock was gone. She had taught me how to persevere during challenging times, and, above all else, to always keep God first. She exemplified all that I wanted to be – a strong black woman who gave back to her family, community, and profession. Most importantly, I remembered her sacrifices to provide for me and my sister.

For a long time, I was grieving and hurting. Life sucked and not having any support from *him* didn't help at all. I decided to remain in New Orleans after my mom's death. He continued to live in Baton Rouge. Our conversations over the next few weeks were rife with arguments about our finances and future. Since moving to Baton Rouge, he still had not secured gainful employment, so to avoid arguments, I paid most of the bills.

During one of those calls in October, he told me he was depressed. I suggested he seek professional help. If he couldn't take care of himself, how could he take care of us? Of me? Days later, I received a call from a social worker at a Baton Rouge mental hospital. He had been admitted.

While he was in the hospital, I sought an attorney to file for divorce. Anxiety and uncertainty consumed me. I didn't want to waste any time. I contacted the social worker at the hospital to inform her that I was going to have the papers served.

He called me crying, asking why I would do this to him? I was not backing down. I was done. He kept calling, but I would not answer. What was there to discuss? After about a week had passed, I finally answered. He begged me to come back. I told him *no*. He could have everything we jointly owned and even assume the apartment lease. Hesitantly, he agreed. I wasn't sure how I was feeling, but I knew this toxic relationship was coming to an end.

Monday, November 19th. We decided this was the day that I would sign over the lease. I woke up early because I had to drive to Baton Rouge. I had a full day planned. First stop, my old apartment complex. Then, conduct a few scheduled in-services. Later that day, dinner with friends.

I was anxious that morning. The hour-long drive to Baton Rouge was quiet. I arrived about 30 minutes before the leasing office opened at 10:00 am and parked my car. Old school jams blared from the car radio as I sang and waited for the leasing office to open.

Out of nowhere, I was startled by a loud knock on the driver's side back window. It was him. He was holding a box containing some work material that I had been asking for. I unlocked the door. He threw the box on the back seat and slammed the door shut. Staring at me through my window, he told me to unlock my door. His eyes were glassy, and he appeared disheveled. I was scared. I didn't want to open the door for him. When I refused, he pointed a gun at me and told me if I didn't open the door, he would kill me.

I pleaded with him to put it away so we could talk. He agreed and placed it in the waistband of his jeans. As I pressed the button to unlock the door, he grabbed the car handle and opened the door himself. I was shaking, sweating, and my heart was beating fast. He told me to get out. I slowly put both feet on the ground and he threw me against the car. He kept repeating that. "if he can't have me, no one else can." He wanted to *kill* me. He was *going to* kill me. But there was no way I'd put my family through another death. He placed his arms around me and dragged me by the blouse towards the apartment. I kicked him and tried to get out of the chokehold he had around my neck. I screamed and screamed and screamed for help. Surely someone must've heard me.

Quickly, he pulled the gun from his waist and pointed it at me. I pushed him away with all the strength I had, and then—

Bang!

There was a loud ringing in my right ear. Had he shot me? He had. He did. I was going to die. I managed to slip out of my blouse. I kicked off my pumps and ran away, frantically looking for anywhere to hide, anyone to help.

My arms were flailing. I was gasping for air. I couldn't look behind me to see where he was.

Bang!

I heard the noise again. I staggered to the ground. I tried to get up, but my legs wouldn't move. I heard voices in the background telling me help was on the way. Help? What could help me now? I needed to get up.

I always used to hear stories of people seeing their life flash before their eyes. I never used to believe it, and I was starting to feel like the biggest idiot because now it was happening to me. I saw my childhood, high school, and college life and recent years had flashed before me. All of it. In the blink of an eye. Then I snapped back.

When the paramedics arrived, they found me lying on the ground in a mangled position. I was conscious, somehow. I had an indescribable pain around my rib cage, a burning sensation in my skin.

The medics moved me on a trauma board, which only worsened the pain. To help me breathe, they stuck oxygen tubes in my nose. They kept messing up the IV infusion, so I told them to forget about it.

They loaded me into the back of the ambulance. There were so many machines, so many supplies. I remember speeding through the streets. The high-pitched sirens. I was crying. Begging the paramedics to tell me what had happened. When I woke up, I was in ICU.

Yes, yes, that's where I was when I first started the story.

There was a gauze bandage taped to my right lower jaw. Why was it there and not near my ear? I hesitantly rubbed my fingers over the bandage and felt a small bump but no blood. But then there was this pain, this *searing, aching* pain in my legs. And there was also this unfamiliar tightness circling underneath my rib cage. I clenched my teeth to keep myself from screaming. I needed my nurse. Now!

Finally, she walked past the curtain, introduced herself, checked the IV lines, and emptied my catheter. It suddenly hit me that I couldn't feel if I had to go to the bathroom or not. Evening visiting hours were nearing. The nurse told me my loved ones were waiting downstairs. I needed to see them, and I'm sure they needed to see me.

They arrived two at a time. The worry on their faces mirrored mine, and for some, there was a moment of relief just to see me alive. We cried, joked, and prayed for healing and a quick recovery. The last visitors left for the day. I was alone again in the cold, noisy ICU room. Before the end of her shift, my nurse brought my pain medication, hoping this would bring me some relief.

As she turned around to leave, I asked her if she knew what had happened to my husband. Her eyes looked down. She took a deep breath and shook her head. Apparently, he didn't make it. After shooting himself at the scene, he was taken to the ER, where he later died from his injuries. She had no other details, and I had no other questions. The meds started working, and I dozed off. I didn't dream that night.

Early the next morning, my doctor walked in, his hands tucked into the pockets of his starched white coat. Calmly, he explained what had happened when I arrived in the ER.

I asked about my face, and he confidently described the entrance and exit wounds. The good news was that there would be minimal scarring, so plastic surgery wouldn't be necessary.

Still, a nagging fear lingered in my mind—that something else might be wrong. That's when he told me about my legs.

In technical terms, he explained that my spinal injury was classified as T6-7 complete, meaning I had lost all voluntary motor and sensory function below my rib cage.

Put simply—and cruelly—the bullet had severed my spinal cord. I was paralyzed and would likely never walk again.

The rest of the conversation was a blur. My mind was fixed on the word "paralyzed," and I began to cry and cry and cry.

Knowing there was nothing more he could say to ease my pain; the doctor left my room. Within a few months of each other, I had lost my mother, my marriage, and now my ability to walk. What did my future hold? Did God still have a plan for me?

It was Thanksgiving Day when I was transferred to a different room on the floor. Later that day, my case manager stopped by to discuss my next step: moving to a rehabilitation facility once I was stable. After careful consideration, I decided to relocate to The Institute for Rehabilitation and Research (TIRR) in Houston, Texas. Having family there made it the best choice for me.

However, I had to wait a full six weeks for a bed to become available. Glory be to the United States healthcare system. In the meantime, I had to wait, and that by itself was a painful experience. I had to relearn so many things that I had taken for granted – bathing, dressing, toileting, and transferring out of the bed. It was all so much. I didn't think I'd ever return to normalcy. My legs were so heavy. I didn't have the strength to lift them with my bare hands. The most humiliating thing was the inability to control my bowel and bladder. I cried from embarrassment every time I had an accident. The nurses kept telling me that I would have to learn to handle my bodily functions. My therapists helped me to celebrate my small victories. I did my best to stay optimistic. Most days were harder than others.

Christmas Day had arrived, and my room was bustling with family, friends, and hospital staff. It was time to transfer to my rehab facility. The next morning, the paramedics arrived early for the long five-hour drive to Houston. I was strapped to the stretcher and loaded in the back of the ambulance. I waved goodbye to my loved ones, wishing I could take them with me.

It was the end of shift when I arrived at the rehab unit. There were loud conversations at the nurses' station, but they all waved and gave me a subtle hello to welcome me. My new room was huge, and there were curtains separating each of the other three beds. TVs were turned on different channels, all blending into a low hum. The paramedics transferred me to my bed. I thanked them for taking care of me and they wished me good luck. I tried not to feel insulted by that, but they were right. I was going to need a lot of luck and a whole, *whole*, lot of prayers. And God.

My nurse came in with her stethoscope hanging around her neck. She bombarded me with questions, began the customary routine of taking vital signs, and oriented me to the unit. It was the beginning of the rest of my life. Wait, you're getting bored? Fine, I'll shorten the rest of it.

My rehab team set goals to push me through recovery. I needed to be as independent as possible. Some days, I pushed around the medical complex, navigated ramps, opened doors on my own, and practiced popping-up curbs.

But the biggest highlight of my rehab was when I passed my driving test. I felt *unstoppable*. Week after week, I met my goals, and my discharge date was set. My sister was getting the house ready with the proposed recommendations to make the house accessible. Physically, I was ready. Mentally, I was not sure. I knew the world would not be accessible and having a disability would take resilience and advocacy work on my part. But I knew I could do it. God had my back.

It was time to go home to New Orleans. My nanny accompanied me. She helped out a lot just by being there. It was my first plane ride after my injury, and I was pretty nervous about it. As soon as I got off the plane, I had a small crowd of family and friends waiting with homemade welcome signs. I was glad to be home. Nervous, of course, but glad.

The challenging work had begun. I tried juggling outpatient physical therapy and full-time work. By the time I finished my morning routine of bathing and dressing, I was exhausted before I even left the house. Many mornings, I cried and grieved. I couldn't do it all, so I resigned from my job. I started seeing a psychologist. The new me was difficult to manage, and I felt so alone. No one around me understood. All they saw was me smiling and pushing my wheelchair.

So, I put all my time and energy into my outpatient therapy. Many patients in therapy were men with spinal cord injuries. A few were training for upcoming wheelchair races, which piqued my interest. I stepped up my weight training, increased my pushups on the parallel bars, and added distance to propelling my chair to get ready for my first 10K.

April 1992, I took part in my first Crescent City Classic. It was a stormy morning. I lined up at the starting line with the other female participants and waited for the horn to blow to begin the race. As I approached mile three or four, I was tired, but quitting wasn't an option. I completed the race in under 45 minutes and won a prize of $250.00. This was a big accomplishment. Finally, I felt there were no limitations due to my disability.

I accepted a part time position as a nurse auditor, then took my first post-injury trip to Cancun. The next year, in the summer of 1993, I went on a cruise with my nanny and friends. On that very first night, I met my future husband.

"And that's what happened," I said.

"Mommy," the little voice in the booster seat behind me said, "You didn't die?"

I was stunned, and it seemed as if the world had stopped for a few seconds. I then

replied, "No, I didn't."

About the Author

After a near fatal injury, Nelita Manego-Ramey has been a steadfast advocate for people with disabilities. She has served on the board of directors of several non-profit and city organizations. Living in an ableist world has brought on many challenges, but it has not stopped her. Nelita has competed in wheelchair races, traveled far and near, and popped waves while water skiing on the Pearl River Canal in Louisiana.

Nelita's natural resilience has enabled her to come through this catastrophic injury unscathed. When not working as a registered nurse, she embraces the culture of her city, New Orleans, reveling in the local festivals, eateries, and cheering on the local sports teams.

After years of thinking about writing her journey as a disabled person and confronting her past, she finally completes her debut story. It gives an account of her life before and after her spinal cord injury.

Manego-Ramey is a graduate of Louisiana State University. She is an active Diamond Life member of Delta Sigma Theta Sorority, Incorporated. Nelita is a widow and has a daughter, Samantha.

How to Connect with Nelita:

https://nelitamramey.org/
Email: info@nelitamramey.org
Instagram: @mysammy
LinKedIn: Nelita Manego Ramey, BS, RN

Acknowledgements

Writing about one of the darkest times in my life was far from easy. Many times, I felt like giving up, but God's wisdom and guidance kept me moving forward and gave me the strength to finish this journey.

To my mother: You were the embodiment of strength and courage during the toughest times. Because of your example, I am the woman I am today. Rest in Heaven, Queen—you are forever in my heart.

To my late husband, Rahn: You always believed in me and told me I could do it. Once again, you were right. Thank you for your unwavering faith in me.

To Samantha, my amazing daughter: Your encouragement and thoughtful feedback helped bring my story to life. I love you more than words can express.

To my village: Your unwavering support has been my foundation through this journey. I am deeply grateful and truly blessed to have each of you in my life.

Thank you to Welcome To The Storm Publishing, and especially Kebra Moore, for your vision and for giving me the jumpstart I needed to bring this dream to fruition.

Finally, to my readers: I am overjoyed to share this story with you. Your support means everything to me. Hold on tight—this is just the beginning!

Carolyn Marshall-Covington, Contributing Author

Educator and Beauty Product Developer
Founder, Insightful Visionaries- 501(c)(3)
Ambassador, Foundation Fighting Blindness
Beacon V.I.P. (Visually Impaired Person)

Unveiling the Real Assignment

Where in the hell did everyone go? My Story

I may have lost my sight, but did everyone around me vanish, too? Once, I was in high demand, surrounded by opportunities and voices calling my name. Now, there's only silence and absence where there was once an overwhelming presence. How did I end up here? For years, people would say I was a force to be reckoned with because I played a pivotal role in driving the empowerment and beauty of women, teaching them to embrace the finer details and celebrating themselves. Yet now, the standards I championed seem to have faded, leaving behind a world that no longer echoes with the same purpose or recognition for me.

My entire journey has felt like a race constantly in motion, a series of milestones to reach and boxes to check off. One assignment after another. I was born on July 2, 1960, to Lewis and Adele Marshall and was one of four children whose journey started in Washington, D.C., before my parents migrated to Glenarden, Maryland.

Glenarden is more than just a place; it's a community with a story of resilience and triumph, a historically Black neighborhood in Prince George's County. It was one of the few places where African Americans could purchase homes and establish thriving neighborhoods, despite segregation and discriminatory housing practices. This backdrop of strength and defiance against the odds has shaped much of who I am today.

My parents were the foundation of my understanding of perseverance and possibilities. My father, a bus driver for the DC Public School System, transported children labeled "*handicapped*" in those days. Today, we say "*disabled*," recognizing their humanity more fully. He would come home and share stories of the children he transported to school, speaking with such empathy for each child. It was in those moments that I first began to understand how varied and beautiful the world is in its diversity. Learning early on that people are different and have different abilities profoundly shaped how I interacted with people for the rest of my life.

All through grade school, I was an average student. But my teachers made sure they left little notes on my report card for my parents. Saying things like, *Carolyn exemplifies outstanding leadership qualities.* I'd flash a big, proud smile until they kept reading. *However, she talks too much. Entirely too much.* My little smile would fade, and my mom would just shake her head and say, "I sure hope you get paid one day for all that talking you do." (Spoiler alert: *She wasn't wrong.*)

My mother, on the other hand, was a trailblazer in her own right. As a housekeeper for wealthy Jewish families, she approached her work with a business mindset, tracking expenses, filing taxes, and running her life and ours with an entrepreneurial spirit. Her unique approach and trustworthiness opened doors to other opportunities.

Sometimes, I pretended to be sick so I could go to work with my mom. She worked with families in the Georgetown area, and their homes always seemed like something out of a magazine. She would give me small tasks, like shining the silver Shabbat candlestick holders and Kiddush cups, little things like that to keep me busy.

Going into those homes, filled with fine art, high end furniture, and home libraries, was like stepping into another life. I knew I would have to work day and night to afford a home like the ones we cleaned, but that didn't matter to me. I still wanted one. I even imagined having my own housekeeper.

See, I didn't necessarily want to be rich; I wanted to live a rich lifestyle.

Dreams and Determination

I'm a big dreamer! As a child, my dreams were so big that people thought they were fairytales. I dreamed of becoming a famous hairstylist, traveling around the world, and owning a chain of salons. While other little girls played house or imagined fairytales, my mind was filled with thoughts of beauty and business. Though there was one thing I wanted more than anything… hair. I didn't have much of it, and it upset me deeply.

My Aunt Christine, whom I affectionately called Aunt Chrissy, tried to console me. She said, "Baby, you got personality, and it will take you a long way in life."

I remember thinking to myself, *Who is she talking to? Personality? I wanted hair like everyone else.* Little did I know how Aunt Chrissy's words of encouragement would impact me throughout my life.

My mother, the resourceful problem solver, found a way to temporarily fix my hair situation. One day, I watched as she cut her own hair to create a ponytail just for me. She attached the ponytail to the top of my head, stepped back, and looked at me. "Now you have hair," she said.

That moment was transformative. It wasn't just about the hair itself; it was about feeling whole because now I felt *seen*. It ignited a spark in me, a passion for beauty and self-expression that would shape my future.

Sometime later, I told my mom I needed a vanity; I just had to have one. She managed to find me a white and gold, full sized vanity. Sitting in front of that mirror, I talked to my reflection for hours, building confidence and practicing the persona I wanted to project. Little did I know how those conversations with my reflection would evolve and shape me into who I am today.

When I was 14, my friend, Penny, and I went to the movies to see *The Omen*. As we left the theater, two women stood outside. One of them said something to my friend, but what stayed with me was what the other woman said to me: "You will become famous and live a long successful life, but something traumatic will happen to you that will alter the trajectory of your journey." Her words unsettled me. I remember thinking, *This is why old folks say, don't talk to strangers.*

At the time, I dismissed it, but those words lingered, their meaning becoming clearer as the years passed. Not that I believe in that kind of stuff, but my face did land on the front cover of *Black Passion International Hair Magazine*. One of the first black hair magazines of its kind in the world. So, I guess I did become a little famous. How about that!

Growing up, I was fortunate to have mentors who believed in me and nurtured my talents. My first mentor was Annette 'Dino' Johnson, a neighbor who lived just three houses up. I admired her hairstyles, makeup, and high-fashion clothing. She drove a Corvette and a Cadillac and just happened to be a hairstylist. That's when I knew I wanted to become a hairstylist, too.

I couldn't wait to go to the 7th grade, to attend Thomas Johnson Jr High, but after two weeks, we were bused to an older school, Beltsville Junior High. The school had 800 students, approximately 600 White and 200 Black, and very few teachers that looked like me. My experience was anything but welcoming. We all, as students, learned about racism really quickly. I became deeply disillusioned with school and going to class, and to no surprise, my grades suffered.

The opportunity came for one person to attend Bladensburg Vocational High School for a 3-year program focusing on cosmetology. The rules required you to be a straight A student and have prefect attendance. I certainly didn't fit the profile. The guidance counselor summoned my mom and me to the office to tell us he was going to break the rules and allow me to participate, saying I was definitely not college material. At the very least, he figured I could learn a trade and just become a worker. At that time, many teenage girls were getting pregnant and relying on government assistance, and he didn't want me to end up like them. I had mixed emotions about what he said. At first, I was upset. However, in the end, I was grateful to have been chosen to go.

My mother, on the other hand, was furious. But I made her a promise. I promised her I *wouldn't* become a statistic. I would prove him wrong. Instead, I would become a successful businesswoman, and that's exactly what I set out to do.

That experience is one of the many reasons I work so hard as an advocate for single moms, making sure they have the support and resources to break free from the system and build better lives for themselves and their children.

I still remember the day I received my little blue suitcase, a cosmetology kit, the tools that unlocked my future. I immediately became a mobile salon in the neighborhood, practicing on everybody, for a small fee of course. One of my first clients was my baby sister, Vanessa, who became my hair model. I'd sit her in front of my vanity, giving her "professional" hairstyles while she cried and made faces as if being tortured.

After school, I caught the T18 Rhode Island bus, heading to work at Audrey's Hairstylists. Audrey Ward, the owner, was my second mentor and became a pivotal figure in my life and career. During the three years I was an apprentice there, I had to grow up fast. I learned how to work with an elite group of clients and discovered that hair salons were a safe space. A place where women came for both a shampoo and therapy.

After completing high school, I landed a job at Bubbles Salon on 2020 K Street NW in Washington, D.C. I chose to work at a chain salon because it allowed me to learn the commission-based structure, which I knew would be valuable when managing my own future chain of salons.

Bubbles had 21 stylists, and I was the only African American stylist. The rest came from a variety of different nationalities. It was my first real experience of being a part of a true melting pot and I loved every minute of it.

A few years later, I returned to Bladensburg, Maryland to work at Fran's Beauty Salon, which happened to be directly across the street from my Alma Mata high school, because I didn't go to college, remember? Fran's was a small personable salon but while working at Fran's, I realized that I couldn't become a famous hairstylist. So, when Fran decided to retire and sell the salon, she offered me the option to buy it. I jumped at the opportunity. Kaywana, Faye, and I worked day and night to raise the money.

Kaywana and Faye were my two assistants. They handled receptionist duties, shampooed clients, and prepped them for me to style. I couldn't have managed without them. Together, we serviced a minimum of 25 clients a day. The community support was tremendous! My neighborhood friends and their families paved the way to launch the first InFlight salon.

My oldest brother, Michael, had just graduated from Yale University with a master's degree in architecture and generously offered to design the salon for free. It was an incredible gift. Thank God because I was fresh out of money. He gave me the start I needed to be successful.

My cousin, Butch, a carpenter by trade, was instrumental in constructing the salon. With his work bag and a small radio, he spent hours each day building the space that turned my vision into reality, and for that, I am forever grateful.

InFlight wasn't just a salon; it was a *groundbreaking* business, the first of its kind for many reasons. We provided my top stylists with opportunities for education, training, and travel as they accompanied me while I worked with major manufacturers such as Gentille, Revlon, and Soft-n-Free. Some even earned the chance to own their own InFlight hair salons.

My team and I created the D'zire hair care collection, which became an international brand. We traveled extensively, training and educating stylists on the product line.

We trailblazed from Maryland to Virginia on to North Carolina, opening more salons. My success wasn't just about talent, it was about *intuition*. I had a knack for identifying potential, and my team was always the most elite in the business. I also knew when it was time to move on to the next assignment.

Upon arriving in North Carolina, I somehow managed to slow down just long enough to marry the love of my life, Dr. Connell Covington. Together, as he built his medical practice, we raised our two sons, Justin and Andrew, while I continued to cultivate and expand my beauty empire.

When I moved to North Carolina and launched Inflight, I didn't embark on the journey alone. Soon after, my dear friend and beauty industry comrade, Kaywana, made an incredible leap of faith, relocating her entire family - Reggie (husband), Kiyana, Brendon, and Trevor - to North Carolina to help grow the Inflight chain of salons.

By 2000, I had expanded my dream to include a day spa. I finally got a seat at the table. It was because of Kaywana that I found the confidence to take an even bolder step to open "Jolie The Day Spa," a venture completely new to me. Stepping into the unknown was daunting but knowing she was by my side made all the difference. Together, we were a force, unstoppable, fearless, and ready to redefine beauty and wellness. I became a co-owner of "Jolie The Day Spa" in Cameron Village. Our location in Raleigh was one of the three spas; one was in Bethesda, Maryland and the other in Buckhead, Georgia. I was under the tutelage of Bernard "Bernie" Condelli, learning the business world from the best! Under Bernie's guidance, what I gained could have equated to an MBA.

I was finally able to open doors for minorities, creating opportunities. We scaled from zero to $1 million in revenue during our very first year, proving that diversity is not just a value but also a powerful driver of growth and success.

One of the most valuable lessons I learned in business during this time was the importance of having an exit strategy from the start. What I didn't realize, however, was that my business partners had already planned to be part of an acquisition. As a result, all three salon and spa locations were being purchased for $6 million. I owned 49% of the Raleigh location, while they held the controlling 51%. I was a drag along, which means I couldn't have stopped this sale if I wanted. After struggling so hard to establish ourselves, especially in Cameron Village, it was a bittersweet moment. But there was something else I was also silently dealing with, my vision loss, something I wasn't ready for them to know. So, as I pressed down to sign the deal, a big smile spread across my face. Not because of the sale, but because in that moment, all I could think about was my school guidance counselor, the one who doubted me, who thought I should just learn a trade and settle for being a worker, I had to laugh to myself.

Life Happens

At the height of my career, the unthinkable happened, my sight began to change, and my world started to dim. It began with small incidents like hitting a mailbox while driving. One incident stands out vividly in my memory. I was driving my dream sports car, a champagne colored with a chocolate soft top 450 SL Mercedes, a car I had worked hard to afford. Somehow, as I was pulling into my garage, the same one I pull into every day, I tore the side mirror right off. Afterward, I simply sat there, stunned, taking a moment to understand what had just happened. It wasn't just the damage to the car that unsettled me; it was the realization that something was wrong.

Seeking answers, I underwent a series of tests at UNC Medical Center. The tests revealed a diagnosis of ***retinitis pigmentosa***, a rare inherited eye disease with no cure. Imagine my devastation upon receiving this diagnosis. The doctors couldn't predict how quickly my sight would deteriorate, it could be weeks, months, or years. In the end, it took years, but the eventual loss was shattering.

There were many chronic eye diseases in my family, some documented and others left undiagnosed. My great-grandfather was blind, although it was never officially recorded. My mother lost her sight and was diagnosed with glaucoma, a condition that marked her struggle. Despite these family ties, blindness was never something I considered for myself. As far as I knew, I was young and healthy or so I thought. It never crossed my mind that my own vision could become part of this painful legacy.

Life was unfolding in unexpected ways. I was quietly dealing with the change in my vision when I suddenly found myself in another situation that I wasn't prepared for, attending my mother's funeral. Adele G. Marshall, that 'G' must have stood for 'GIANT' because that's what she was in my life. I don't recall much about that day, yet I remember everything all at once. It was a cool, rainy Friday afternoon in Virginia as I stood in the aisle of First St. Paul Missionary Baptist Church.

I slowly approached the casket to see my mother. Moving, yet motionless, I found myself standing there, gently twirling her soft, silver hair, and thinking about how beautiful she looked. I loved my mother's silver hair; they had styled it so beautifully. What I remember most about that day was the overwhelming feeling of wanting so badly to talk to her. I wanted to tell her, "Momma, it's okay. It's okay being blind. I will be able to live my life." But I never uttered a word.

My mother was concerned about me living in the darkness that she wanted to escape for so long. As my vision continued to diminish, I found myself wanting more and more to talk to her about what I was going through. Each time the subject came up, she shifted the conversation to her own experiences, how greatly she wanted her sight back, and her hope for a cure. She had undergone several procedures in hopes of restoring her sight, but none were successful. I had one conversation with my mom about the possibility of it being hereditary, but it didn't go very far. Like many families, we avoided discussing medical issues, and in the end, nothing more was said.

Let me be clear, I loved my mother dearly even though she never ever talked to me about losing my sight. I believe it was tied to her feelings of guilt, a guilt rooted in a mother's instinct to shield her children from every harm, even the things beyond her control. She must have hoped, perhaps prayed, that this burden would somehow skip my generation, sparing me from the struggles she knew too well. Not talking about it was her way of coping with me losing my sight, and it weighed on my heart, leaving me to wrestle with the uncertainty alone. I can't begin to fathom the weight she carried, the sleepless nights wondering if there was something, anything she could have done to change my fate. It was an unspoken question, left unanswered, that lingers to this day.

By 2015, my world was turned upside down in a single moment. During a doctor's appointment, I was officially declared "legally blind." In an instant, everything I had was taken away from me. I could no longer drive; no longer move with the independence and freedom I had known for so long. I was suddenly in a space where I had to figure out how to live, how to adjust, how to even begin to cope with the gravity of what was happening.

If I'm honest, I had already been living with the impairment for some time but managed to continue functioning and building my beauty empire, believing that by the time I accepted it, there would be a cure. Hearing the words spoken aloud and knowing they had been put in writing was a weight I couldn't escape. There was something *final* about it. The doctor's declaration made it *real* in a way that nothing else had. The loss, once subtle and gradual, now felt permanent and undeniable. What made it even harder to bear was knowing there was no cure, no treatment, no chance of reversal. It wasn't something that could be fixed, not with time, not with money, not with medical intervention. At least that's what I believe based on what I was told at that time.

Losing your sight isn't just a physical challenge; it's an emotional and existential one. It is dealt with in three distinct phases: denial, grief, and acceptance. I was truly in denial, so I rebelled.

Rebellion comes with a price, and I paid mine through a series of embarrassing mistakes. Once, I accidentally climbed into the wrong car, startling an elderly woman, a situation that could have gone terribly wrong. Another time, after leaving a movie, I patiently waited for my husband to come out of the men's restroom. Mistaking a stranger's silhouette for my husband, I grabbed his arm and began walking with him. I'm not sure what happened next or what the man's expression looked like, but I vividly remember my husband's voice cutting through the confusion. "She's blind! She's blind!" The man and his wife were understandably upset.

I don't know what embarrassed me more, my husband announcing my blindness to the world or being seen as a Jolene, a husband-snatcher. Either way, it is something I'll never forget. These moments forced me to confront the truth I had been avoiding. I realized then it was time to isolate myself from the world and come to terms with my reality.

Denial gave way to grief. I retreated into isolation, spending over a year and a half in my wine cellar with my little dog Remy. Thinking of all the things you think about when you create space for it. How will I care for my husband, my children, my family? My employees? How can I work? How am I going to pay my bills? Why me? Yeah, me. How will I, oh my God, how am I going to take care of me?! I have worked so hard my entire life, now what?

Isolation and Transformation

My inner voice asked, *Did everyone around me vanish, too?* The disappearing act that I speak of is when you realize there is no one around. After being in the business for over 40 years, training and serving thousands of employees and clients, not to mention having the same house and cell phone numbers for years, only a faithful few continued to check on me. I understood how fast the world moved but you mean to tell me that there wasn't a moment to call or check in?

It's difficult to put into words the unspoken feeling I carry around every day. Looking in the mirror, but she does not look back. I miss seeing myself. Me. My face in that mirror. Closing the door and hearing nothing other than my voice speaking to me.

Then, one day, something shifted. I heard my quiet voice speak certain words I didn't expect to hear, "You can sit here if you want to. The world is moving on." I realized that I could stay stuck in this space of silence, or I could stand up and fight. One day, I heard a pastor on the radio say, "That everything that happens to you is FOR YOU… the good and the bad and we must give thanks in all of it." I then started thinking to myself how God has blessed me. Blessings just fell on me. I cannot take credit for anything that I've done in life. It has always been a faith-driven journey.

Acceptance and Advocacy

It didn't happen overnight, but eventually, I stopped resisting. Denial and grief gave way to a tentative acceptance and with that came a new chapter in my life.

Once you have been classified as *disabled*, you are placed in the "system." What system you may be wondering? The North Carolina Division of Services for the Blind system. They began reaching out to offer support services, but I wasn't ready to accept any. It seems as though they were calling every day. When I would answer the phone and realize it was them, I would say, "You've got the wrong number," or "She's not available", clinging to denial.

Rehabilitation services sent an intake and interview specialist to my home. The first thing they wanted to do was send me to a shrink. I firmly told them, "No, no thank you! I've never seen a shrink before, and I'm not about to start now. I've been listening to everyone else's problems all my life." They were talking to me like I didn't know how to solve problems.

So, then, they sent a mobility specialist to train me on how to use a cane. She kept asking if I wanted to walk to the mailbox. "No, I don't walk to mailboxes," I sharply replied. The specialist acted like something was wrong with me. There was nothing wrong with me. My refusal was rooting in my understanding, and that was walking to that mailbox wasn't going to fix anything. I was *unwilling* to accept this new reality and vowed never to use that big, ugly white cane. But eventually, I did.

Next, they sent me to the Raleigh Lions Clinic for the Blind, a community of people who understood my struggles in ways others could not. It was there that I met Steve Murphy, a fellow traveler on this journey who shared the same rare and incurable disease. Steve showed me what was possible, not through lectures or coaxing, but simply by being himself. His life was proof that blindness was not the end; it was a new beginning. One of his favorite sayings is, "There is life after blindness." But he never mentioned a cure. No one ever mentions a cure.

Another pivotal figure in my journey was Lee Davis, my instructor, a man whose resilience and wisdom were even more profound because he, too, was blind. Lee didn't just teach me; he helped me rediscover my confidence at a time when I needed it most. With his guidance, I learned to navigate cutting edge technology and adaptive equipment designed for the visually impaired. His patience, expertise, and unwavering support made all the difference, empowering me to embrace tools that unlocked new possibilities for independence.

As I immersed myself in this training, something within me shifted. I transitioned to a stronger, more resilient mental and emotional space, one where I no longer saw my blindness as a limitation but as a new way of moving through the world.

Then, just as I was beginning to find my footing again, I received a phone call from Tim Johnson of Tim Johnson International. His words took my breath away. I had been nominated for the Living Legend Award at the Beauty and Barbers United Gala. The news washed over me like a wave of validation. In that moment, I felt alive again. The beauty industry, the world I had poured my heart into had not forgotten me. This recognition wasn't just about an award; it was a reminder that my impact still mattered, that my story was still being written. I had six weeks to get myself together. I needed a complete beauty overhaul. Ebony, Michele Green-King, and Essence Heel, my glam squad, stepped up and put me back together.

In 2016, I founded Insightful Visionaries, a 501(c)(3) nonprofit dedicated to empowering people with disabilities. Just as InFlight Salons filled a void in the beauty industry for Black women, Insightful Visionaries sought to fill a void for people in the disability community, like me, who wanted more. When I realized there were very few programs or business development opportunities for the visually impaired, I knew something had to change.

Society often misses the opportunity to work with blind individuals because they perceive visual impairment as a negative. However, blind people are some of the most innovative and remarkable individuals you will ever meet and work with. Visually impaired people are incredibly creative because they first see it in their mind, then help the world see their creativity through the sighted eye.

Through Insightful Visionaries, I created programs and events that shattered stereotypes. One of the most groundbreaking was Blind Idol, a national singing competition for visually impaired individuals started by Chris Flint and Anastasia Powell, who worked for Industries For the Blind (IFB) of Winston Salem. In June 2017, I had the opportunity to host this competition.

Competitors flew in from across the country to participate.

The highlight of the evening was our guest artist, Matthew Whitiker. We sought Whitaker after his April 2017 performance on the *Ellen Degeneres Show* and *Fox's Showtime at the Apollo*, where he won first place.

Blind Idol became so popular that it went viral on social media, catching the attention of *American Idol's* legal team. They sent me a cease-and-desist notice, threatening legal action if we continued to use the word "Idol." I was stunned. I forwarded the letter to my son, who was in law school at the time, to review it. "Mom, they're serious," he said. "You'll need a lawyer."

I laughed and replied, "That's why I sent it to you. I was hoping to get the family discount." Ultimately, I passed the notice along to IFB's in house counsel to handle.

Later that summer, I was gearing up for my birthday tradition. Every year, I would go to the beach and invite friends. Two things I could always count on, one is a call from my friend, Alvin Massenburg, and two, Kaywana always showing up. This year in particular, Kaywana wasn't sure if she could make it to Myrtle Beach due to a scheduling conflict. I reassured her that it was perfectly fine and told her not to stress about coming. Still, after some rearranging, she made it happen, and we celebrated as usual.

Before she left, we did what we always did, reminisced, sang songs, and laughed like we had for years. It was in one of those quiet moments that I felt her looking at me. Kaywana said, "Your blindness is no mistake. You are blind by God's divine purpose. He has a new assignment for you, and you had better write a book! And if you don't I'mma be mad at you!" I smiled, we shared a laugh, and those moments passed like many we'd shared before. Then, she left.

Three days later, the phone rang. It was the kind of call that makes the world stand still. My dear friend of 40 years was gone; she had passed away in her sleep. Just like that, I would never hear her voice, her laughter, or her words of encouragement. Her passing left me with a numbness and a host of unanswered questions, but above all, it stirred something deep within me. What was the assignment she believed God had for me? What did she see that I couldn't?

I never had the chance to ask Kaywana what she was talking about or even if she fully understood, but as my life unfolded, I reflected on how life's challenges could shape me into a vessel of service. I now realize that blindness, rather than being a limitation, is a unique calling to help others facing similar circumstances.

My mission as a blind individual is rooted in recognizing my God-given purpose to uplift others in similar situations. The first step in fulfilling this mission was establishing a nonprofit to provide resources, training, and a community for blind individuals, enabling them to live independent and fulfilling lives. Insightful Visionaries has since become a hub of empowerment, offering skills training, assistive technology, and emotional and spiritual support.

Through this work, I have come to understand that my assignment is not just about building a nonprofit, it is about inspiring others to see their value and purpose. God's assignment for me has been revealed as a journey of service, advocacy, and faith, showing that physical blindness does not equate to spiritual or visionary blindness. I am a living testimony of how God uses perceived weaknesses as strengths to fulfill His greater plan.

This book shares the message that everyone, regardless of ability, has a role in God's vision for the world. As 2 Corinthians 12:9–10 reminds us:

"But he said to me, 'My grace is sufficient for you, for my power is made perfect in weakness.' Therefore, I will boast all the more gladly about my weaknesses, so that Christ's power may rest on me. That is why, for Christ's sake, I delight in weaknesses, in insults, in hardships, in persecutions, in difficulties. For when I am weak, then I am strong."

Serving others often brings deeper clarity about God's assignment for our lives.

Ask yourself: What challenges in your life might God be using to reveal your true assignment?

Building Bridges and Breaking Barriers

Insightful Visionaries was just the beginning. Over time, the organization expanded to include the DIVA's Alliance. What is a Diva? A woman with Diverse abilities, Inspirational, Victorious, and Accomplished. This network was designed to foster a sisterhood environment where every woman, regardless of ability, could thrive and make a meaningful impact.

As my work continues, I will reflect on the lessons I've learned. One of the most valuable lessons learned is the importance of giving. Someone once asked me, "What gift do you think you inherited from your parents?"

The answer was simple: "The gift of giving." My mother had an open heart and was always willing to help those in need. I carry that legacy with me in everything I do.

Looking Back and Moving Forward

Over the span of 40 years, my accomplishments have been many. I've been a licensed cosmetologist, an instructor, salon, spa. and school owner, mentor, ambassador, advocate, and nonprofit leader. I've employed and mentored over 1,500 people, helping many of them start their own businesses. I've balanced the demands of having a career, raising two sons, and maintaining a strong marriage. I have to say, I am fortunate and grateful to have a husband who has not only been present but a provider. He supported me not only in our marriage but in all of my businesses then and now. I couldn't have done any of this without him.

In recognition of my impact, WRAL named me a community role model, and I was inducted into the NC Women Business Owners Hall of Fame in 2020. *I* was the 2024 award recipient of The North Carolina Black Women Empowerment Network, a community partnership award. I am featured in the Foundation Fighting Blindness (FFB) national campaign "Stronger Together."

The Foundation Fighting Blindness is a leading organization at the forefront of the global effort to prevent, treat, and cure blinding diseases. I am honored to serve as an Ambassador for the Foundation Fighting Blindness and as a Beacon V.I.P. (Visually Impaired Person).

My greatest accomplishment is the legacy I've built not in spite of my blindness but because of it. Losing my sight gave me a new perspective on the world, teaching me to prioritize what truly matters and inspiring me to fight for a future where everyone, regardless of ability, has the opportunity to succeed.

I hope that each person reading this book will appreciate and embrace each of the women in this book that has willingly shared their stories, struggles and triumphs. Their journeys are a testament to resilience and strength.

As I look to the future, my mission remains clear. I want to continue breaking down barriers, building bridges, and inspiring others to live boldly. After all, I may have lost my sight, but I've never lost my vision for helping others.

About the Author

Carolyn Marshall Covington is a dedicated business professional with extensive expertise in salon and spa ownership, management, and personal empowerment. With over 40 years of passionate service in the beauty industry, Carolyn has employed over 1,500 people, many of whom have gone on to become successful entrepreneurs, celebrity stylists, and educators. She is considered a role model and a beacon of success in the hair industry. Carolyn's career began with the Inflight Hair Salon, which blazed a trail from the DC/MD area to North Carolina, opening a multitude of salons. She and her team developed D'zire haircare and traveled worldwide, educating stylists around the world. Her frequent travels and studies abroad enriched her knowledge and led to the inception of her dream salon.

From salon owner and platform artist to educator and product developer, Carolyn's self-driven and highly motivated professionalism has propelled her to the top of her craft. In 2000, she realized her dream by opening Jolie the Day Spa in Cameron Village, which provided opportunities for minorities to enter the day spa industry. In 2002, that same year, Carolyn faced a significant personal challenge when she was diagnosed with Retinitis Pigmentosa (RP), a degenerative eye disease. Despite this, she remained undeterred in her mission to make a difference in the lives of others.

After undergoing rehabilitation and adjustment, Carolyn founded Insightful Visionaries, a 501(c)(3) non-profit organization dedicated to empowering persons with disabilities. Guided by her faith, she embraced this new phase of her life, using her experiences to help others. Insightful Visionaries relies on grants and donations to support its programs for individuals with disabilities, and Carolyn's leadership has been instrumental in its success. She was inducted into the North Carolina Women Business Owners Hall of Fame in 2020 and serves on the Raleigh

Mayor's Committee for Persons with Disabilities. Additionally, she is a keynote speaker, Advisory Board member of Enterprising Women, and actively involved with the North Carolina Council of the Blind and the Governor Morehead School for the Blind Alumni Association.

Carolyn has come full circle to her love for the beauty industry with CEO Haircare System, aiming to cultivate the best conditions for hair growth. Her vision is to make people feel beautiful inside and out, and she has created an affiliate program to promote generational wealth for those who share her products with friends and family. Although she has lost her sight, Carolyn has not lost her vision for helping others. She continues to encourage women business owners and individuals with disabilities to achieve their highest potential through events, knowledge sharing, and unwavering support.

How to Connect with Carolyn:

https://carolynmarshallcovington.com/
Email: info@cmcspeaks.com
FB: @inspirationaldvocate
Instagram: @cmcinspirationaladvocate
LinKedIn: Carolyn Marshall Covington

Acknowledgements

I am deeply thankful and grateful to be a daughter, sister, niece, cousin, auntie, wife, sister-in-law, stepmother, mother, Godmother, and a proud Gigi to four beautiful grandchildren. I now embrace the role of friend and mentor to so many wonderful people in this world. This is just a glimpse of my journey, as there are countless others who have played a vital role in my life.

For 32 years, I have been blessed to be under the leadership of Pastor Kelvin D. Redmond, whose guidance helped me remain humble, accept my blindness, and grow my faith. To my esteemed mentor Pastor Classy Preston, your unwavering love and support have been a guiding light in my life for the past 24 years, and your wisdom, encouragement, and faith have shaped me in ways I could never fully express, as I am forever grateful for your presence, guidance, and the countless ways you have blessed my journey. To my forever friend, Sylena Slaughter, thank you for loving me just as I am. To my Ride or Dies—Renee (Sunshine) 30 plus years of love, once I was leading you now you are guiding me. Tab, Angie, Anthony, Terry, Karen, Sanita, Patti—you have been my pillars of strength, always guiding me when I needed it most. Though I have lost one set of eyes, I have gained the vision of so many others.

I am forever thankful to Bobby Bennett, Gentille Sales and Educational Director, for helping me find my voice in the beauty industry. One of my greatest memories is creating the Dream Team—Flavia, Marion, Tanya, Ralph, and David Byrd (Fashion Designer; RIP)—to perform in London, England. To my business collaborators— Vanessa Jones (sister), Roszetta Pringle, Tabitha Cole, ChaJuan Cox, Liz Armstrong, Shalondra Cooper, Dorothy Wooten, Mary Newton, Michele Green-King, Tammy Wells, Ta'Modge, Kim Pishock (RIP), Matricia Bellamy, Anna Crooms, and Kim Best you have made this journey unforgettable. To my original beauty baby, Reecy, even though your wings were clipped early, you rose to every challenge with courage and resilience.

You inspired me more than words can express. Aretha, thank you for being a faithful "traveling" employee for every NC salon I have ever possessed. You are like my second shadow, looks like we are stuck together. Thank you, Tonya Ridley, for being the ultimate Inflight Van chauffeur, skillfully driving with lightning speed to get us to Durham every day and back. Thank goodness we are still here, we survived. Marcia, Thank you for reaching out to me and sending well wishes on every holiday. Donna, "Peewee," our relationship is a true testament to the bond we share. Thelma (Smiley), your heart is as big and warm as your smile. Dallas, thank you for the energy you share with the beauty industry. Together, we shine and make magic. Thank you, Pamela Bullock, for trusting me with the development of the Studio 10 hair care product line. To my CEO Haircare Team—Carlos, Kelly, Mary, Graham, Sauls, Arnetta, Anita, Melissa, Dejanay Caffey, and Tiera—together, we will change the dynamics of the beauty and barber industry. To Sherrod Halloway and Torres Harris, I thank you both so much for all the partner collaborations we completed.

To anyone who has been a part of my village, mentoring you has been my greatest success. Customer care has always been a priority. We are so thankful for all of the customers that have supported us over the last forty years.

To my Insightful Visionaries team—Dr. Paula Smith-Sawyer, Steve Murphy, Wendy Coulter, Andrew Covington, *Esq.*, S. M. Kernodle-Hodges, and my personal assistant, Stephanie Jones—your dedication inspires me every day. Thank you to all Insightful Visionaries supporters and the blind community for standing by me. To Jason Menzo, CEO of FFB, your faith in me allowed me to shine as a star and speaker in the "Stronger Together" commercial. Lastly, my heartfelt thanks to S. M. Kernodle-Hodges for turning my life story into a beautiful masterpiece.

To the visually impaired community—your courage, perseverance, and determination continue to inspire the world. Never let anything dim your light or limit your vision for success. You are seen, valued, and capable of achieving greatness. Keep striving, keep believing, and know that you are never alone on this journey.

Rev. Dr. Raedorah C. Stewart, Contributing Author

Womanist: Poet, Preacher, Narrative Theologian (Storyteller)
Professor: World Religions, Critical Thinking, Academic Writing

Loop, Hook, Pull: Disabled by Design– Creating a Narrative Theology of Disability!

As a disabled person, Psalm 139:13-14 has long presented as theologically problematic for me. How could, *"For you formed my inward parts; you knitted me together in my mother's womb. I praise you, for I am fearfully and wonderfully made. Wonderful are your works; my soul knows it very well,"* fall as praise from my lips when as young as six years old, I realized I was differently abled, and that's with all the shameful, negative connotations assumed with being so. My theological narrative about disability centered on the sins of the mother, shame of the family, pity of the public, and sympathetically low expectations for achieving, excelling, and fitting into mainstream ableism.

This article weaves biographical vignettes and theological reflections to develop a liberation hermeneutic for creating a narrative theology of disability in the Church; challenges commonly held perceptions about disabled personhood; examines familiar efforts to enhance the worship experience for disabled persons; admonition of practices that inconvenience or otherwise undermine a disabled parishioner; and the efficacy of ministry accommodations to equip disabled persons to worship, serve, and lead in the Church.

Disabled at Birth and By Accident

At six years old, I first felt the crushing weight of shame as I recognized my profound stutter. As both a stutterer and an undiagnosed neurodivergent child, I lived in a world that seemed determined to misunderstand me. Strangers would stare and snicker during my struggling speech, schoolmates turned my differences into daily torment, and even my family members made my challenges the subject of relentless teasing.

I embodied a perplexing contradiction, devouring Reader's Digest magazines and acing vocabulary quizzes by age ten while avoiding childhood games. The cacophony of my large, boisterous Southern family overwhelmed my senses, yet my retreat into solitude was seen as problematic rather than protective.

All I yearned for was acceptance of my natural way of being, to engage with the world without it assaulting my body, mind, and spirit. Instead, I faced an endless barrage of demands: act normally, socialize more, behave better. I learned to navigate life's waters alone, bearing the weight of invisible yet insidious disabilities. Shame became my constant companion, a shadow that followed me through every stuttered word and sensory overwhelm, as I learned the art of suffering in silence.

For decades, I managed my stutter through intensive speech therapy, mastering breathing techniques, and cognitive strategies. Then, at 50 years old, a single moment on the ski slopes shattered everything. The crash not only wreaked havoc on my musculoskeletal system but resulted in an acquired brain injury (ABI) from the impact on my motor cortex. This plunged me back into the profound stuttering of my childhood. Before I could fully comprehend the extent of my spinal and musculoskeletal injuries or the long path of rehabilitation ahead, my voice betrayed me first.

The acute stuttering returned vigorously, breaths that produced no sound, F's, M's, and T's that caught and snagged on my tongue like wool on thorns, and vowels that dissolved into mere whispers before they could escape my teeth. Suddenly, I was that shame-filled six-year-old again, only now accompanied by debilitating anxiety that required medication and would herald the next decade of rehabilitation. As a preacher and teacher, my livelihood depended on the very thing that now betrayed me—my voice.

Psalm 139:13-14, words that had once brought comfort, further presented a spiritual crisis. *"For you created my inmost being; you knit me together in my mother's womb. I praise you because I am fearfully and wonderfully made."* How could I reconcile these words with my stuttering tongue and injured brain? How could I see divine intention in my broken speech, divine wonder in my neural miswirings?

During my recovery, between nerve studies and physical therapy sessions, I found solace in crochet, my hands creating something beautiful while waiting for medication to dull the pain. One day, as I worked on pink roses for children who had lost their mother to breast cancer, my fingers choreographed a familiar dance of loop, hook, and pull, and *divine understanding* finally broke through. The yarn in my hands became a metaphor for God's creative work, not just in those deemed "perfect" by human standards, but in *all of us*: in my stuttering speech, in my compromised mobility, in their mother's BRCA1 gene.

The biblical image of God knitting suddenly transformed before me. Like crochet, each perceived imperfection, each "dropped stitch" in human form, be it a stutter, a genetic mutation, or an injury, was part of a larger pattern, a *divine artistry* beyond our limited understanding. This revelation challenged the prevalent theological narrative that equates divine favor with physical perfection, ability with excellence, and wholeness with flawlessness. Instead, I found a new theology emerging from my hands' work: one that embraces the full spectrum of human experience, where even our perceived imperfections are threads in God's masterpiece.

Disabled *Imago Dei*

The Church's narrative around disability remains stubbornly resistant to transformation, despite powerful biblical precedents. Consider Mephibosheth in 2 Samuel 4, born able-bodied, disabled through injury, exiled because of his disability, yet ultimately restored to his rightful place at the King's table while remaining disabled. Or reflect on the man born blind in John 9, whose parents bore the weight of assumed sin, only to become Jesus' chosen vessel for teaching divine purpose in disability.

Yet these stories, rich with implications for disability theology, often gather dust in our pulpits and liturgies. For those of us living with disabilities, the church experience frequently offers three bitter options: face the coercive pressure of healing lines where our faith is measured by our willingness to be "fixed," endure the subtle violence of pitying glances and whispered prayers, or fade into invisibility within spaces designed for the able-bodied. The message is clear: our bodies and minds are problems to be solved rather than expressions of divine creativity.

But imagine a revolutionary reading of Psalm 139:13-14 that embraces disability as another facet of the *Imago Dei*. Picture a theology that recognizes *divine blessing* isn't contingent on meeting society's narrow definition of sensory normalcy, having eyes that see, ears that hear, tongues that speak without stumbling, hands that feel without tremor, feet that walk without aid, minds that process in expected ways, or emotions that conform to prescribed patterns. This theological shift would do more than liberate those of us with disabilities from the crushing weight of internalized shame; it would dismantle the unspoken hierarchy that suggests God favors the able-bodied. Such a transformation would finally align the Church with legal, cultural, and academic progress in disability rights and accommodation. Instead of merely tolerating our presence, the Church could embrace the full spectrum of human ability as a reflection of divine creativity. This isn't about installing ramps or providing large-print bulletins, it's about fundamentally reconceiving disability as a sacred variety rather than divine punishment or a problem awaiting a solution.

What do you truly know about the people with disabilities in your church beyond their names and the origins of their disabilities? Have you taken time to understand their unique needs, learning about the physical accommodations that could transform their worship experience from challenging to inclusive? Look around your leadership, where are their voices, their gifts, their influence? When you envision the future of your congregation, do you see disabled members as vital contributors to its growth and vitality? Most crucially, how do your church's storytellers, your pastors, preachers, ministers, teachers, leaders, and congregants, portray disabled personhood in your community's narrative?

These questions aren't merely rhetorical exercises; they're doorways to transforming your church's narrative theology of disability. Consider this: if we genuinely believe that each person reveals another facet of God's nature, then viewing disabled persons as essential to your church's story and mission isn't optional, it's *vital* to experiencing God's full expression in your community. This mirrors the profound truth of 1 Corinthians 12, where unity doesn't mean uniformity, and every gift, every variation of human ability, enriches the whole body of believers. But transformation demands more than a mere census of disabled members or a checklist of accommodations. It requires commonly abled pastors and leaders to invest deeply in knowing disabled persons as true equals in faith and family. This means moving beyond surface-level inclusion to genuine relationships, beyond tolerance to celebration. For just as a crocheted tapestry gains its strength and beauty from each unique loop, hook, and pull, God has woven us all through the same divine love into one family in Christ and Creation.

Scooters, Sidewalks, and Saints

Living with disabilities means carrying exhaustion that able-bodied people rarely comprehend, a bone-deep weariness from constantly navigating a world that wasn't built with us in mind. When I connect with other disabled individuals, whether in person or through social media, our shared laments often center on the daily gauntlet of attitudinal, structural, medical, and financial barriers that drain our energy and limit our movement through the world. Two spaces where these challenges hit me hardest are urban sidewalks and churches, places that should offer connection but often present obstacles instead.

Take the urban landscape, where shared bikes and scooters have become the latest challenge in our obstacle course of daily life. In my vision of an accessible world, these vehicles would be equipped with technology to prevent careless abandonment, particularly near crucial access points like curb cuts and ramps. But the reality is far different. What might seem a minor inconvenience to others, a scooter left tilting across a sidewalk, a bike sprawled near a ramp, becomes a formidable barrier for those of us navigating with wheelchairs, canes, or other mobility aids. For my visually impaired friends, these scattered obstacles become dangerous trip hazards. For my neurodivergent community, who rely on predictable paths and routines, these random barriers trigger waves of anxiety and distress.

The most frustrating part? Watching able-bodied pedestrians step nimbly around these obstacles, unseeing and unthinking about their impact. It's not that they're deliberately cruel; they simply haven't had to calculate each step, haven't had to turn back or risk injury because someone's convenience became our barrier. This unconscious ableism reflects a deeper societal blindness to disabled experiences. It's not enough to simply blame individuals, we need systemic change. We need cities to implement and enforce strict regulations on shared mobility companies, requiring designated parking areas that don't impede accessibility. We need public awareness campaigns that help people understand how their small actions can have enormous consequences for others. Most importantly, we need a fundamental shift in how society views accessibility, not as an afterthought or special accommodation, but as a basic right that benefits everyone. When we create truly accessible spaces, we create a world where all of us can move freely, connect easily, and live fully. This is an opportunity for the church to take the lead in disability justice.

The church claims to be a sanctuary for all, yet for those of us with sensory sensitivities, traditional worship can feel more like an assault than an embrace. Every Sunday, I navigate a gauntlet of sensory challenges: thunderous music that pierces rather than uplifts, lighting that sears rather than illuminates, and well-meaning physical contact that sets my nerves jangling. The dreaded "passing of the peace" transforms a moment meant for connection into an exercise in survival, each unexpected touch, each close encounter, and each burst of sound pushes me closer to sensory overload.

I have learned to protect myself by remaining seated during these moments, choosing stillness over overwhelm. But this choice comes with its pain, the whispered judgments, the sidelong glances, the labels of "unfriendly" or "antisocial" that stick like burrs to my reputation. If only they could understand that my physical withdrawal isn't a rejection of community but a desperate attempt to stay present in it.

My love for my faith family runs deep; it's the sensory tsunami that I can't navigate. It took years to find my voice and to gather the courage to be vulnerable about my needs. When I finally spoke with my pastor and church leaders, explaining my sensory experiences, it felt like stepping out onto thin ice, would I fall through or find solid ground? To their credit, they listened. Now, when I lead worship, I do so from the pulpit, offering waves and blown kisses instead of handshakes and hugs. It's different, yes, but no less genuine, no less connecting.

Yet, individual accommodations, while vital, is just the beginning. I dream of churches that embrace sensory diversity as naturally as they do musical styles, spaces where multiple paths to participation exist side by side. Imagine worship services with designated quiet areas, thoughtful lighting design, and touch-optional greeting practices. Picture a community where diverse needs aren't just accommodated but celebrated as part of our divine diversity.

This isn't about making church comfortable for people like me, it's about transforming our understanding of what true inclusion means. When churches lead the way in embracing sensory diversity, they become catalysts for broader societal change, demonstrating that accessibility isn't a burden to be shared but a gift to be unwrapped together.

Do More, Do Better

"Reasonable accommodations", these words echo through public spaces, academic halls, and corporate offices like a hollow promise. As someone who has navigated these accessible spaces, I've learned that "reasonable" often translates to "minimal," defined by what's least expensive for owners and least disruptive to the able-bodied majority. It's a checkbox approach to inclusion that satisfies legal requirements while failing to truly welcome disabled persons into full participation. The Church cannot afford to settle for such tepid reasonableness. Our call is to radical inclusion, a transformative welcome that reimagines our facilities, programs, leadership structures, and spiritual formation through the lens of full accessibility. We're not called to do what's reasonable; we're called to do what's right.

Let me share one pathway toward this radical inclusion: Consider how we typically approach sign language interpretation in worship, a volunteer interpreter is often relegated to the margins of both physical space and video frame, serving sporadically when available. Now imagine expanding this into hosting sign language interpreter internships and partnering with professional training programs.

This isn't about providing more consistent interpretation; it's about weaving deaf accessibility into the very fabric of church life. These interpreting interns would serve for three to twelve months, becoming familiar faces in our community rather than occasional visitors. They would bring professional-level skills while gaining invaluable experience in religious interpretation. More importantly, their consistent presence would signal to deaf and hard-of-hearing believers that they aren't afterthoughts, they're essential members of our faith family.

Think bigger: This partnership could become the foundation for a vibrant deaf ministry within a traditionally hearing congregation. Each interpreted service and each accessible program become another strand in a tapestry of inclusion, drawing more deaf believers into our community. What begins as an internship site could blossom into a full-service deaf ministry, transforming our church's story from one of mere accommodation to one of true belonging. Like the artful process of crocheting, each small loop of progress leads to another hook of opportunity, pulling through new threads of ministry until we've created something beautiful and strong, a church where accessibility isn't just reasonable but radical.

When churches claim to mourn their growing "sick and shut-in" list while neglecting basic accessibility, they reveal a profound disconnect. As someone who has faced these barriers firsthand, I know that many "homebound" members aren't choosing isolation, they're being excluded by our failure to provide basic access. Think about it: how many of those on your prayer list would be active participants if they could simply enter the building with dignity?

Let's be clear: ramps, lifts, and designated seating aren't "special accommodations," they're as fundamental as the front door. Yet, too often, I watch churches treat these essentials like optional luxuries, their maintenance relegated to the bottom of budget discussions with sighs and eye-rolls. For disabled believers like me, these features are our running shoes, our basic equipment for participating in the race of faith. A cracked sidewalk or malfunctioning automatic door isn't a minor inconvenience; it's the difference between worship and isolation.

The tragedy deepens inside our sanctuaries, where even those of us who manage to enter face another kind of barrier, the well-intentioned but traumatic demands for spontaneous interaction. Since my acquired brain injury, I've learned to dread those moments when a preacher suddenly commands, "Turn to your neighbor!" For those of us with cognitive and mental disabilities, these forced interactions aren't fellowship, they're minefields. What looks like standoffishness to others might be someone desperately managing sensory overload, fighting back an anxiety attack, or struggling to process multiple social demands at once.

Imagine if we approached church accessibility with the same dedication we give to other aspects of ministry. Regular maintenance of ramps and lifts should be as routine as changing the altar cloths. Smooth, crack-free sidewalks and reliable automatic doors could transform our "sick and shut-in" list into an active membership roster. Most crucially, reimagining our worship practices to embrace multiple ways of participating, making physical contact optional, providing quiet spaces, and allowing people to engage at their own pace, could make our sanctuaries truly sacred spaces for all.

Like the intricate process of crocheting, each small improvement becomes another loop in the fabric of inclusion. When we repair that cracked sidewalk or install that automatic door, we're not just fixing infrastructure, we're creating pathways for full participation in worship, Bible study, and leadership. By understanding that accessibility isn't an expensive "extra" but a fundamental expression of our faith, we can transform our churches from spaces of exclusion to sanctuaries of true welcome.

When you see us seeming withdrawn or distant, please understand we're often not being antisocial, we might be adjusting to new medication or quietly fighting to prevent an anxiety attack in public. Creating a culture of explicit consent around touch rather than treating physical contact as a mandatory expression of faith, would transform our experience of worship.

It would allow us to participate in these moments of communal affection in ways that honor our boundaries rather than shame us into mimicking the able-bodied majority. Think of it like crocheting an afghan: making touch optional is the first loop, respecting personal boundaries is the hook, and creating space for unusual ways of expressing fellowship pulls us toward a deeper trust in the community. When we're not ostracized for needing measured stimulation, we can finally believe that God's people utterly understand and accept our invisible disabilities.

While this appeal barely scratches the surface of needed changes, here's where you can start, look around your congregation for those of us already in your midst, though perhaps on the margins. Seek out our perspectives, invite our ideas, and support our deeper involvement. Use our lived experience as the foundation for developing an intentional plan to welcome others with disabilities and their families into full participation in congregational life. Remember, we're not asking for special treatment, we're asking for the opportunity to worship, serve, and belong in ways that acknowledge our full humanity. By making these changes, you're not just accommodating disabilities, you're enriching the entire body of Christ.

To Do and Not To Do

For the church to truly embrace disability justice, we must move beyond mere accommodation to radical inclusion. As someone living with disabilities, I've experienced firsthand how well-meaning churches often perpetuate harmful attitudes while believing they're being helpful. Let me share some essential guidelines that could transform your church's approach to disability:

- First, banish the phrase, "But you don't look disabled," from your vocabulary. When you say this to me or others with invisible disabilities, you're not offering a compliment, you're questioning the validity of our lived experience. Such comments carry an implicit accusation of fraud, deepening the isolation we already feel.

- The casual use of "crazy" as a descriptor for anything chaotic or unusual must stop. As someone with mental health challenges, I wince every time I hear this word thrown around in church settings. It's not just insensitive, it's a weapon that's been used to shame and silence people like me for generations.

- When you move a wheelchair user to a pew to make space for liturgical dancers or holiday decorations, you're sending a clear message about who belongs in your sacred space. Imagine being asked to check your legs at the door because they're "in the way", that's exactly how it feels to us.

- Understanding our need for consistent seating goes beyond comfort, it's about access and dignity. When I choose a particular seat, it's not preference but necessity: it determines whether I can hear the sermon, see the worship leaders, or exit quietly if needed without drawing attention to myself.

- Leadership training becomes truly inclusive when you simply ask us what we need: it's transportation assistance, sign interpretation, or a learning partner. Provide these supports with joy, recognizing them as investments in the full expression of God's gifts in your community, not burdensome obligations.

- Finally, create a special needs ministry that's shaped by special needs individuals. Invite us to train your volunteers. Let us design the programs. Our lived experience is your greatest resource for understanding how to serve the disability community effectively. These changes aren't about making church more accessible, they're about recognizing that disability justice is central to the gospel message. When we truly embrace all bodies and minds as bearing God's image, we create a church that reflects the full diversity of God's creation.

Disabled Ability

We who live with disabilities are not God's afterthoughts; we are intentionally and purposefully crafted expressions of divine artistry. To be disabled is to be abled differently, each of us fearfully and wonderfully made, our disabilities woven into the fabric of our being. We are God's marvelous works, not despite our disabilities but with them, each of us a unique embodiment of the *Imago Dei*. When I speak of being disabled with abilities, I'm not describing a paradox but a profound truth: our unique ways of moving through the world are part of the rich tapestry of human experience. Let me share a testament to this truth. I stand among a cloud of witnesses, a paraplegic Rabbi, a blind Deacon, and me, a preacher who stutters and a seminary professor living with an acquired brain injury. While some might view us as exceptions, we're simply living examples of what's possible when determined self-advocacy meets meaningful support.

Yet, ironically, our greatest challenges often arise not in academia but in the church itself, where an unspoken theology of "survival of the fittest" still whispers that God's favor rests primarily with the non-disabled.

Even as we've labored to reclaim Psalm 139:13-14, embracing our fearfully and wonderfully made selves, we've had to forge our paths to ministry rather than finding the church eagerly making space for our gifts. Many of us serve quietly, our disabilities undisclosed, haunted by the fear of shame and exclusion. We've seen too often how our differences can become weapons against our opportunities for leadership and full participation in congregational life. Like any group of people, we span the full spectrum of abilities and gifts. Some of us excel at practical tasks, others bring brilliant theological insights or engineering solutions. The key isn't categorizing what we can or can't do, it's honoring each person's unique calling and creating spaces where those calls can be answered. When a pastor leads their congregation in developing a theology of disability, it transforms inclusion from an afterthought into a fundamental aspect of ministry.

Picture a church that sees itself as incomplete without the voices of disabled persons at every decision-making table, where commonly abled members naturally create the space and pace we need to be fully heard. Imagine a community that recognizes how much poorer it would be without our unique perspectives and contributions. Like the intricate process of crocheting, each of our loops, hooks, and pulls is essential to creating the tapestry of God's kingdom. The Church isn't truly whole until it embraces all its members, disabled and commonly abled alike, as integral threads in the divine design.

A New Narrative

While churches may be legally exempt from ADA compliance, our spiritual mandate runs far deeper than any legal requirement. As someone living with disabilities, I know that true inclusion will only emerge when the Church embraces a radically different narrative, one that sees us not as divine afterthoughts or human mistakes but as *intentionally crafted* expressions of God's creativity. Imagine each disabled person as an essential thread in God's magnificent tapestry, our presence adding depth and texture to the divine design through our unique loops, hooks, and pulls. Our differences aren't flaws to be fixed but sacred variations to be celebrated. When I declare, "I am fearfully and wonderfully made," I'm not speaking despite my disabilities but through them, each limitation and adaptation are part of God's marvelous work.

My deepest hope is for a day when Psalm 139:13-14 evokes images of wholeness that transcend conventional abilities when both disabled and commonly abled believers can join in full-throated praise, recognizing that God's image shines equally through all forms of human experience. Let us work toward that day when our churches don't just accommodate disability but *embrace* it as essential to the full expression of divine creativity when every stuttered word, every wheeled entrance, and every signed prayer is recognized as its form of sacred poetry.

Suggested Resources:

Bessey, S., & Chu, J. (Hosts). (n.d.). *Evolving Faith* [Audio podcast episode]. In *Identity, Belonging, and Disability.* Evolving Faith. https://evolvingfaith.com/podcast/season-1/ep-17?rq=disability

Coleman, M. A. (2016). *Bipolar Faith: A Black Woman's Journey with Depression and Faith.* Fortress Press.

Melcher, S. J., Parsons, M. C., & et al. (n.d.). *The Bible and Disability: A Commentary (Studies in Religion, Theology, and Disability).*

Pratt, M. (2018). *Salt and Light: Church, Disability, and the Blessing of Welcome for All.* Twenty-Third Publications.

Stewart, R. C. (Host). (2021). *WGBD: When God is Black & Disabled* [Audio podcast]. http://www.wgbd.blog, https://podcast.app/wgbd-when-god-is-black-and-disabled-p1901188

About the Author

The Rev. Dr. Raedorah C. Stewart (she/her) is a multifaceted leader who inspires the world as a preacher, poet, professor, painter, writer, and narrative theologian. A devoted mother and champion of inclusivity, she serves as Artist-in-Residence and Worship Leader at Covenant Baptist United Church of Christ (SE Washington, DC). As the Faculty Director of the Writing Center at Wesley Theological Seminary (NW Washington, DC), she equips seminarians in academic writing and publication, and she teaches religious studies at Tennessee State University (Nashville, TN).

For over two decades, Stewart has contributed to the American Academy of Religion, serving on committees like Womenism and Society, Black Theology, and Disability in the Profession. Her work spans peer-reviewed journals and faith-based blogs, exploring disability and faith, queer studies in religion, and theology in the arts. She also fosters community through her podcast, *WGBD: When God is Black & Disabled*, where Black women of faith share their experiences with disability and chronic illness.

As a published poet, Stewart has shared her creative spirit through two self-published poetry collections and individual commissioned poems in other theology and ministry textbooks. Further enriching the world of worship, her forthcoming book, *Hear the Spirit: Ritual Poems and Radical Litanies*, arrives in 2026 from Wipf&Stock Resources. Stewart's academic journey includes a Doctor of Ministry in Spirituality and Story from Wesley Theological Seminary (Washington, DC), and a Master of Arts in Christian Leadership from Fuller Theological Seminary (Pasadena, CA).

Fun Fact: I am a porphylophile (lover of purple), wear purple every day, and have curated a perfectly purple peace-filled home.

How to Connect with Raedorah:

Email: raedorah.stewart2@gmail.com
FB: @RevDrRaedorah
LinKedIn: revdrraedorah

Acknowledgements

I give God thanks and praise for everyone who has made accommodations for me beyond the legislated guidelines for persons with disabilities. Your ability to see my humanity, worth, purpose, creativity, giftedness, and brilliance because of rather than in spite of, my disabilities allows me to live authentically and unapologetically.

I dedicate this work to my care team and network: psychiatrists, therapists, community support workers, neurologists, nurse practitioners, physical therapists, chiropractors, cardiologists, electrophysiologists, ER physicians, EMTs, nurses, dentists, employers, colleagues, professors, students, drivers, concierges, my pastor, my congregation, and friends who know when to push me out the door and when to simply check on me in bed.

I sincerely hope to always bear witness to your love and kindness towards me.

Natalia Trota Gerald, Contributing Author

Children's Author
Founder, Inspire Her Books
Founder, DPTV Tango LLC
Military Veteran

The Invisible Struggles:

A Journey of Strength, Self-Discovery, and Being Dyslexic!

Definition of Dyslexia

*D*yslexia is a learning disorder that primarily affects the ability to read, spell, write, and sometimes speak. It is characterized by difficulties in recognizing and decoding words, despite normal intelligence and adequate educational opportunities. Dyslexia is not related to vision or intelligence but rather stems from differences in how the brain processes language.

What Doctors Say About Dyslexia

1. **Neurological Basis:** *Dyslexia* is a neurodevelopmental disorder. Doctors and neuroscientists describe it as resulting from differences in brain structure and function, particularly in areas involved in language processing. These areas may include:

   - The left hemisphere of the brain.

   - Regions responsible for phonological processing, word recognition, and memory retrieval.

2. **Symptoms and Diagnosis**: Common signs include:

   - Difficulty reading accurately and fluently.

   - Problems with spelling and writing.

- Challenges in decoding (breaking words into sounds) and phonemic awareness. Diagnosis typically involves assessments by psychologists, educators, or speech-language pathologists.

3. **Coexisting Conditions:** Dyslexia may coexist with other learning or attention disorders, such as Attention-Deficit/Hyperactivity Disorder (ADHD). However, it is distinct and requires specific interventions.

Genetic Aspect of Dyslexia

Doctors and researchers highlight the genetic component of dyslexia:

- **Heritability:** Dyslexia often runs in families. Children with a parent or sibling with dyslexia are at higher risk of having the condition.

- **Genetic Variations:** Studies have identified specific genes associated with dyslexia, such as DYX1C1, KIAA0319, and ROBO1, which influence brain development and language skills.

- **Environmental Interactions:** While genetics play a significant role, environmental factors, such as exposure to language and reading opportunities during early development, can influence the severity of dyslexia.

Treatment and Management

Dyslexia cannot be cured, but it can be managed effectively through:

- **Educational Interventions:** Structured literacy programs and phonics-based approaches.

- **Assistive Technologies:** Tools like text-to-speech software or audiobooks.

- **Therapies:** Speech and language therapy to improve processing skills.

- **Support Systems:** Encouraging parental and teacher involvement for emotional and academic support.

By understanding dyslexia as a genetically influenced, neurologically based condition, doctors emphasize the importance of early diagnosis and tailored interventions to help individuals succeed.

Common Signs Associated with Dyslexia

Dyslexia can affect various aspects of learning and daily life. Below is a list of common disabilities or challenges linked to dyslexia, many of which I have experienced firsthand:

1. **Reading Difficulties** - Problems with decoding words, fluency, and comprehension.

2. **Writing Challenges** - Difficulty organizing thoughts, spelling errors, and poor grammar.

3. **Spelling Problems** - Frequent misspelling and trouble recalling letter sequences.

4. **Processing Speed** - Slow processing of written and spoken language.

5. **Memory Issues** - Struggles with short-term memory and recalling sequences like numbers or directions.

6. **Time Management Difficulties** - Problems estimating and managing time effectively.

7. **Directional Confusion** - Mixing up left and right or difficulty with spatial orientation.

8. **Attention and Focus Problems** - Difficulty sustaining attention, especially during reading or writing tasks.

9. **Phonological Awareness** - Trouble recognizing and working with sounds in words.

10. **Mathematical Challenges** - Struggles with arithmetic operations and number patterns.

I saw myself in nearly every description listed above. I frequently reversed letters and numbers, found it challenging to retain written instructions, and often needed more time than others to process information. Reading aloud remained an intimidating task, and spelling continued to be a hurdle no matter how much I practiced.

Recognizing Struggles

For most of my life, I battled feelings of inadequacy as I struggled to make sense of my difficulties with reading, writing, and processing information. As a child, I often felt out of place, watching others excel while I lagged. I convinced myself that trying harder would fix everything. But no matter how much effort I put in, the struggles persisted.

I vividly remember sitting in class, staring at a page that seemed to shift and blur. My teacher's voice called on me to read aloud, and panic shot through me. My throat tightened, my hands trembled, and the words tangled in my mouth as the classroom filled with whispers and stifled laughter. I wanted to disappear. But that moment planted something in me—an ember of determination that I refused to let burn out.

When I first arrived in the United States in 1984 from the Philippines, my challenges were compounded. English was my second language and attending a public military school only amplified my struggles. My inability to keep up was dismissed as a language barrier. I believed it, too, for years. It was easier to blame my struggles on learning English rather than confront the idea that something deeper might be wrong.

Words often looked like jumbled puzzles, impossible to decipher. I couldn't keep up with the pace of lessons, and the pressure to perform weighed heavily on me. I fell behind, repeating kindergarten, but I refused to let that define me. Instead, I pushed myself harder, determined to prove that I belonged.

Reading comprehension was one of the most confusing challenges I faced. I would read passages multiple times—sometimes three or four—just to make sense of the content. Breaking down sentences into smaller parts was the only way I could retain what I had read. Even then, I often needed to stop and reread entire sections, making it difficult to keep up with lessons and assignments.

Writing was not easy. My sentences lacked structure, and spelling errors littered my work despite endless practice. Assignments that took my classmates minutes to complete would take me hours. Studying felt like climbing a mountain with no end in sight. Yet, I kept climbing.

Tests were always my biggest enemy. No matter how much I prepared, the anxiety never left me. I could feel it in my chest before every exam— the pounding heart, sweaty palms, and the voice in my head reminding me of past failures. I hated that feeling, but I faced it repeatedly.

I learned to expect failure, but I never let it stop me. If I failed a test, I studied harder and took it again. Retaking tests became normal to me. I didn't enjoy it, but I saw it as part of the process. I kept pushing because I refused to let one test define my worth.

Preparation became my armor. I joined study groups, always seeking out the smartest person to learn from. I asked questions, practiced relentlessly, and developed routines that worked for me. I broke down information into manageable chunks, used flashcards, and relied heavily on repetition. Reading aloud became one of my tools for memorization, and I wrote out key information repeatedly to reinforce it.

I also leaned on extra credit. Even when I struggled in a subject, I found ways to improve my grades. I knew I had to work twice as hard, so I took every opportunity to stay competitive. If there was extra credit, I completed it. If there was an alternative way to earn points, I found it. I refused to fall behind.

Despite all my preparation, the anxiety never disappeared. No matter how much I studied, I couldn't escape the fear of failure. But I learned to push through it. I accepted that fear would always be there, but it didn't have to control me.

In elementary school, I attended speech therapy, which helped a little with language development. But even with that support, no one recognized the signs of dyslexia. I continued to struggle, feeling like I was carrying a weight that no one else could see.

Recognizing Dyslexia Later in Life

I didn't even know about dyslexia while I was going to school. The first time I heard of it was when I joined the military. While studying in the medical field, I learned about learning disabilities, and it made me think— I could be dyslexic.

Realizing that dyslexia might explain my experiences was both validating and overwhelming. It reframed my past struggles—not as personal failures but as challenges rooted in a learning difference. This new perspective allowed me to better understand myself and explore tools and techniques to manage these challenges.

Before this revelation, I often noticed how I said phrases out of order and blamed it on English not being my first language. My first language is Tagalog, and even then, I wasn't sure if I was speaking it correctly. Growing up, I struggled to retell stories if someone asked me to. I could only repeat what I thought was the correct version, often feeling uncertain and frustrated with myself. It felt as though the details got jumbled in my mind, and I second-guessed what I heard, no matter which language I was using.

School was especially tough. I often felt like I was falling behind, even when I worked hard. I watched my peers grasp concepts quickly while I wrestled with the simplest instructions. Reading out loud felt like walking on a tightrope—terrifying, because I knew I might trip over words. Writing wasn't any easier. Letters and words seemed to move around on the page, and my spelling often looked nothing like the words I was trying to write.

This wasn't just about academics—it was about how I saw myself. I carried an unshakable feeling that I wasn't "enough." Teachers, friends, and even family sometimes assumed I wasn't trying hard enough or wasn't paying attention. But the truth was, I was giving it everything I had. I just didn't know why my brain seemed to process things so differently.

Learning about dyslexia was like someone flipping on a light in a dark room. It gave me a name for the struggles I had faced my whole life and, more importantly, a *reason* behind them. I wasn't lazy or careless—I was *dyslexic*. That realization changed everything. I began to see that my challenges didn't mean I was less intelligent. They just meant I needed different tools to unlock my potential.

Looking back, I'm grateful for the resilience I developed, and now I know this is one of the reasons I always felt why I thought I was always different. My experiences have taught me to be patient with myself and to approach challenges with creativity and determination. They've also deepened my empathy for others who may be struggling silently, as I once did. Today, I embrace dyslexia as part of who I am, and I use it as motivation to push forward, knowing that I have the strength to overcome whatever comes my way.

Mixing Up Numbers and Letters

One of the most frustrating challenges I faced was mixing up numbers and letters. If someone gave me a phone number, I often reversed the digits or wrote them down out of order. The same thing happened with letters when taking notes or copying information. This created *anxiety* and *embarrassment*, especially when I had to ask people to repeat themselves multiple times.

To manage this, I started rewriting the numbers or letters several times until they looked right. I also began double-checking my notes and repeating information back to others to make sure I got it correct. While it didn't eliminate the problem, it gave me more confidence and control over my work.

During my active years in the military, these challenges became even more apparent. One of my roles was working at the front desk, where I received messages. This was incredibly stressful for me. When someone called, I had to write down their information quickly, but my brain didn't process the information fast enough for me to take the message accurately while still listening to the caller. If someone was standing in front of me giving instructions or details, I struggled to jot them down without pausing to clarify or asking them to repeat themselves. I sometimes mixed up names, numbers, or times, and I constantly worried about making a critical mistake.

To compensate, I took extra time to write things down carefully, even if it meant slowing down the process. This often drew attention and made me feel embarrassed, as though I couldn't handle a task that seemed so simple for others.

Each setback fueled my resolve. I learned to mask my difficulties, relying on memorization and repetition to get by. I became a master at pretending everything was fine, building walls to protect myself from judgment. But inside, I carried the shame of not being able to keep up. It was exhausting.

What I didn't know then was that my experiences mirrored those of many others with dyslexia. Dyslexia affects an estimated 15-20% of the population, but for years, it often goes undiagnosed, especially in children who speaks multiple languages or come from immigrant backgrounds. The inability to decode words, retain information, and keep up with peers is common among dyslexic individuals, yet it is frequently overlooked in favor of assumptions about effort or intelligence.

Looking back, I wish I had known more about dyslexia and how it shaped my life. It wasn't until much later that I realized my brain wasn't broken—it was just wired differently. The challenges I faced were not a reflection of my worth or abilities but of a learning difference that required understanding and support.

Learning this gave me the tools to manage my difficulties in a healthier way. I began using strategies like breaking tasks into smaller steps, using visual aids, and relying on technology to assist with writing and note-taking. While the challenges haven't disappeared, I've learned to navigate them with more confidence.

Today, I look at my journey with a sense of pride. The road wasn't easy, but it shaped me into someone who is resilient and resourceful. It also gave me a deep sense of empathy for others who might be struggling silently. My dyslexia doesn't define me—it's just one part of the person I've become.

Overcoming Challenges and Building Resilience

Looking back, I'm amazed at how far I've come. The obstacles I faced felt impossible at times, but I refused to let them define me. I didn't have early diagnoses or specialized support systems. What I had was grit, determination, and an unshakable drive to keep going.

Hiding my struggles became second nature. I feared being labeled or seen as incapable, so I worked twice as hard as everyone else. That fear of judgment transformed into fuel, pushing me to prove that I was capable. Every failure became a lesson, and every setback made me stronger.

A turning point came when a friend casually asked if I was dyslexic. For the first time, I let down my guard and admitted it. That moment of honesty was liberating. It wasn't a weakness—it was the first step toward *owning* my story. I began reflecting on my life and realized that my struggles weren't about intelligence; they were about how my brain processed information. Knowing this reframed my past. Instead of seeing failures, I saw victories—the countless battles I had fought and won just to keep up.

I learned that resilience wasn't about never failing—it was about refusing to stay down. I discovered strength in my persistence, creativity, and adaptability. My learning style was different, but it wasn't wrong. Once I embraced this truth, I felt empowered to keep pushing forward.

Joining the military was another defining chapter in my life. It challenged me in ways I had never experienced, but it also gave me structure and discipline. I learned to rely on systems and strategies to overcome my weaknesses. The military didn't lower its expectations, so I had to rise to meet them. And I did. I am proud to say that I am a retired Air Force veteran, having served my country with honor and determination.

Education was another mountain I was determined to climb. Despite the challenges, I not only earned my bachelor's degree, I went on to complete my master's degree and proud to say I graduated with honors. These accomplishments represent more than academic success—they are symbols of my resilience and refusal to let dyslexia hold me back.

Today, I wear many hats. I am a business owner, running multiple ventures that reflect my passions and hard work. I am also a published children's book author, with works available in both English and Spanish. Sharing stories that inspire and connect with young readers brings me immense joy, especially knowing how powerful representation and encouragement can be for children facing their own challenges.

I share my story now because I know I'm not alone. There are others still struggling in silence, and I want them to know that they are more than their challenges. *Dyslexia doesn't define you—how you **rise above** it does.* My journey hasn't been easy, but it's been worth every step. And if my story can inspire even one person to keep going, then every struggle I faced will have been worth it. You are capable, resilient, and stronger than you realize. Don't ever let the world tell you otherwise.

Resources

If you or someone you know is navigating dyslexia, there are countless resources available to provide support, guidance, and empowerment. Understanding the available tools and options can make all the difference in building a successful academic and professional life.

Resources for Dyslexia Support

1. **International Dyslexia Association (IDA)**

   - Website: dyslexiaida.org

   - IDA provides a wealth of resources, from understanding dyslexia to finding specialists and educators who can help. Their focus is on advocacy, education, and early intervention.

2. **National Center for Learning Disabilities (NCLD)**

   - Website: ncld.org

   - Phone: 1-888-575-7373

   - NCLD supports individuals with learning and attention issues, including dyslexia, offering resources for parents, educators, and students.

3. **Understood.org**

   - Website: understood.org

   - This organization offers tools, expert advice, and resources tailored to students with dyslexia and their families, as well as interactive communities.

4. **Decoding Dyslexia**

   - Website: decodingdyslexia.net

   - This grassroots movement provides advocacy and awareness efforts at the state level, connecting families with local support.

5. **Dyslexia Hotline Numbers**

   - Call **LD Online**: 1-888-575-7373 for general learning disabilities support.

   - Contact local dyslexia resource centers in your area; many states have centers specifically for dyslexia assistance.

Scholarships for Students with Dyslexia

Many organizations offer scholarships for students with dyslexia to support their educational journey:

1. **P Buckley Moss Endowed Scholarship**

   - Designed for students with dyslexia or other learning differences pursuing post-secondary education in the arts.

2. **Rise Scholarship Foundation**

   - Focuses on students with learning disabilities, including dyslexia, and awards scholarships based on academic achievements and determination.

3. **Learning Disabilities Association of America (LDA) Scholarships**

   - LDA occasionally offers scholarships for students with learning disabilities, emphasizing education and training.

4. **Anne Ford Scholarship**

   - A $10,000 scholarship offered through NCLD for high school seniors with learning disabilities pursuing a four-year degree.

College Disability Services Programs

When you start college, one of the most valuable resources you can tap into is the school's **Disability Services Office**. Here's why:

- **Accommodations:** These offices provide tools like extended test times, note-takers, and assistive technology to ensure you're on a level playing field with other students.

- **Advocacy:** Staff in disability services can help you communicate your needs to professors and assist with understanding your rights under the Americans with Disabilities Act (ADA).

- **Community:** Many disability services programs offer workshops, peer mentoring, and support groups that connect you with students facing similar challenges.

Tips for Success in College

- **Be Proactive:** Reach out to the Disability Services Office as soon as you're admitted to ensure accommodations are in place when classes begin.

- **Use Assistive Technology:** Tools like text-to-speech software, audiobooks, and specialized apps can streamline your studies.

- **Communicate with Professors:** Don't hesitate to discuss your accommodations with your instructors. Transparency can help them better support you.

Conclusion

Navigating dyslexia can be challenging, but the right resources, scholarships, and support systems make success achievable. Whether you're a student, parent, or educator, remember that help is always within reach. By seeking out opportunities and taking advantage of the programs designed to assist, you can pave the way for a brighter future.

About the Author

Natalia Trota Gerald is a multi-talented entrepreneur, author, and inspiring figure originally from the Philippines, now making her mark in Dallas, Texas. With an impressive educational background, she holds a degree in Health Administration and Business from Wayland Baptist University and an MBA from Phoenix University. Natalia's career began with a 20-year commitment to the U.S. Air Force, where she served in medical management roles across various global locations, including Germany, Hawaii, South Carolina, and New Mexico.

Following her distinguished military service, Natalia founded DPTV Tango LLC, a company that focuses on governance contracts and consulting services for government missions. Now venturing into the world of children's literature, Natalia hopes to inspire young readers, especially girls—to pursue their dreams with confidence, drawing from her own childhood experiences and aspirations.

Outside of her professional pursuits, Natalia is a dedicated community member. She coaches track and field and is an active member of Delta Sigma Theta Sorority, Inc. She volunteers in organizations like the Frisco VFW, American Legion, and Veterans Foreign War Organization. With the support of her husband and pride in her sons, Natalia is excited to motivate the next generation through her storytelling and life journey.

How to Connect with Nalalia:

https://tangobos.com/
https://inspireherbooks.net/
Email: info@inspireherbooks.net
FB: @Natalia Series Book
Instagram: @dptv_tango
LinKedIn: Natalia Trota, MBA

Acknowledgements

This book is a deeply personal exploration of life with a disability, offering an honest reflection on both its challenges and triumphs. Through raw and heartfelt storytelling, I share how my journey has shaped not only my identity but also my relationships with family, friends, and the world around me.

Society often views disability through a lens of limitation, but this book presents a different perspective—one of resilience, creativity, and love. It is a testament to the idea that our struggles do not define us; rather, it is our ability to adapt, connect, and find joy in life's smallest victories that truly shapes who we are.

With the unwavering support of my incredible family, my loving husband, two vibrant sons, and devoted parents, I have learned to embrace life fully and unapologetically. This story is a celebration of love, the power of human connection, and the unbreakable strength that resides within us all. Thank you for joining me on this journey.

Dr. Yvette Pegues, EdD, PhD, Contributing Author

Author, Speaker, Disability Advocate,
Consultant, Inclusion Advisor
Co-Founder, Your Invisible Disability Group
Ms. Wheelchair Georgia, 2014
Ms. Wheelchair USA, 2016
Ms. Wheelchair International, 2018

Foreword

The power of storytelling is transformative. It heals wounds, builds bridges, and gives voice to the silenced. *Our Power* is more than an anthology—it is a testament to the resilience of Black women navigating disability, leadership, and faith. This book is an offering of truth, strength, and hope for those who seek to break barriers and redefine what is possible.

In *Crowns for Christ: A Life Worth Saving*, Dr. Yvette Pegues shares her extraordinary journey from overcoming adversity to becoming an advocate, leader, and trailblazer. From navigating a life-changing disability to winning multiple national titles, her story is a powerful testament to faith, perseverance, and using one's challenges as a platform for change. Her resilience, rooted in faith, continues to inspire, and uplift those striving to defy limitations and build a legacy of impact.

The Exhale – Origin Story

Never in a million years would the child of unschooled immigrants believe that decades later, she would be traveling the world, impacting fortune 10, 100, and 1,000 of companies. That she would disrupt technology, race, gender, and ability barriers. She would find her person and together, create two more incredible people and live a coveted life that was never modeled yet desired. She would have an actual crown placed on her head – not once, twice, but three times. Become the first in her generation to hold a terminal degree and use her life to serve others – in service to Christ.

Many Firsts – I Won't Be The Last

From the very beginning, the odds were stacked against me. Born as the youngest child to immigrant parents, I was also the first of my family's generation to be born on U.S. soil. That duality—being last and first all at once—would set the stage for my life in ways I could never have imagined.

Growing up in South Florida, I was surrounded by a kaleidoscope of cultures, languages, flavors, and traditions. The city was as vibrant as my healthy curiosity. Even as a child, I was an overachiever, always chasing dreams that seemed just beyond my reach. I wasn't content to simply observe the world around me; I needed to understand it. With no formal guidance, I taught myself to read by hunting down every unfamiliar word that I heard on TV and uncovering its meaning in the tattered dictionary on my family's bookshelf.

For me, school wasn't just a place to learn—it was where I felt truly alive. It was where I excelled, belonged, and discovered a haven from life's uncertainties. It wasn't simply a place of education; it was a *lifeline*, one that saved me in ways that I would come to understand years later.

The path hasn't always been easy. Life threw its share of challenges my way, testing my resolve and reshaping my dreams time and time again. But through resilience, determination, and an unwavering sense of purpose, I learned to rise, reaching back and lifting others along the way. As I look back, now, I see how every trial, every triumph, and every twist in my journey was part of a greater plan.

It reminds me of the promise in **Jeremiah 29:11**: *"For I know the plans I have for you," declares the Lord, "plans to prosper you and not to harm you, plans to give you hope and a future."* That verse anchors me. It's a reminder that my story isn't just about me—it's about paving a path for those who will come after me. I may be the first in many ways, but I'm certain of this: ***I won't be the last***.

A Journey From Homelessness To Hope

Only a few knew my secret. Truth be told, at that time, I didn't even fully grasp it myself. After graduating high school, I became unhoused. I thought I just needed a place to stay after being kicked out of my childhood home, but looking back, I see the fragility of those years more clearly. Between the ages of 17 and 19, I lived in a rotation of borrowed spaces— my father's house with his new wife, the cramped side room in a pretend cousin's home, and at my lowest point, a makeshift closet in a real-life crackhouse.

Through it all, I maintained the image of stability. Each morning, I put on a polished façade, burying my struggles beneath layers of professionalism. By day, I dressed in pantyhose and business attire, working as a bank teller in an affluent beachfront community. By night, I balanced jailhouse visits with loved-ones, community college classes, and a shifting dream of becoming a court reporter.

It was a bittersweet time of contradictions and chaos. I carried an innocence that allowed me to push forward, unaware of the weight of my circumstances. My ignorance was more than bliss—it was a matter of survival. Yet, even in the midst of instability, blessings seemed to find me.

Years later, despite my stepmother ruining my credit, I took my first real step toward stability by buying a house from an older woman willing to hold the mortgage. With no windows, no doors, and no air conditioning, that house was barely livable. My first big purchase wasn't furniture or appliances; instead, it was a set of doors to secure my home. I'll never forget the pride I felt while sleeping soundly on an inflatable mattress atop a cold, concrete floor.

Every improvement to that house was a labor of love and faith. I DIYed my way to making it my dream home, one jalousie window and one paycheck at a time. Over time, the house became more than shelter; it became my *sanctuary*. It wasn't just my home—it became a refuge for the mother who once turned me away, a space for healing, and a tangible reminder of how far I'd come. What began as a windowless house became a haven for restoration, hope, and love.

Even in my hardest seasons, I experienced an unwavering provision that can only be explained by grace. **Psalm 37:25** speaks to that truth: "*I was young and now I am old, yet I have never seen the righteous forsaken or their children begging bread.*"

My journey is a testament to the resilience, the faith, and the blessings that find us, even in the most uncertain and broken moments.

Yes, To The Dress: Meeting Him Right Where We Were

Life was good—better than good. Landing the job of my dreams, I relocated from Miami to Atlanta and started traveling the world as part of my new engineering career. It felt like the culmination of everything I had worked for, and finally, I made it to my first IBM conference in Las Vegas, a milestone I was proud to reach.

But life has a way of surprising us. At that conference, I was paired with a mentor who flat-out refused to work with me. His reasoning? He believed a young, female college hire like me would be better matched with a female mentor. Corny, right? I thought so, too. After all, I'd been working in male-dominated spaces for years and knew how to handle myself. To make matters worse, he insisted on addressing me only by my last name.

That might have been the end of it, a blip on an otherwise exciting journey. But then, I noticed that something had changed. He showed up again, as more than a friend, with a blinding engagement ring and an entirely different energy. He offered me a new last name.

Our wedding was as intimate and beautiful as our love. It took place in the backyard of our sprawling 5,000-square-foot home in North Georgia and unfinished basement, purchased just two months earlier. We exchanged vows under an altar overlooking the lake, surrounded by both sets of parents, family members, and special friends. The reception was held on the main floor of our empty, three-story space, perfectly staged for dancing the night away.

Supposedly, 'not each other's type' – meeting and marrying my husband represents the line that separates my life from who I was and the dreams we created together. He is, and always will be, the love of my life—the ice to my fire, the yin to my yang, and the calm voice that reminds me to breathe. I didn't know it then, but God sent him to me with a purpose: to lead me to Christ, to be the father of our children, and to lead our family through the unexpected journey of life that lay ahead.

To this day, the strength of our marriage isn't just in how we complement each other but in our foundation of faith. **Ecclesiastes 4:9-12** sums it up perfectly: *"Two are better than one, because they have a good return for their labor: If either of them falls down, one can help the other up. But pity anyone who falls and has no one to help them up. Also, if two lie down together, they will keep warm. But how can one keep warm alone? Though one may be overpowered, two can defend themselves. A cord of three strands is not quickly broken."*

God, my husband, and I—we're that cord of three strands, woven together in strength, resilience, and purpose. Together, we are better than we could ever be apart.

My Mommy Had Brain Surgery & I'm Okay

It all began as a dream come true—the chance to return to school and break free from the negative cycles of parenting I had learned growing up.

I was determined to follow God's model of parenting. My journey started with a Montessori class that ended with a whole degree in Early Childhood Education. I was eager to be the best possible parent for Isaiah, soaking up every lesson, seeing the difference it made. But, I had no idea how much that decision would shape my parenting and our family's story.

Our second son, Elijah, had a surprise baby shower in the university breakroom. He became a class favorite, spending countless nights in the model classroom. I felt *proud*—proud of what I was learning and proud to know I was giving my children a foundation rooted in love, intentionality, and God's guidance.

Toward the end of my program, my hard work caught the attention of an Ivy League institution for a new terminal studies program. The opportunity was thrilling, and despite juggling work, school, and family, I couldn't wait to take on this new challenge.

Without notice, the right side of my body began to feel off. Then, it felt like fire rushing through my veins. My body was carrying a secret that it could no longer keep. A visit to the emergency room revealed the unimaginable: I was born with a rare *brain malformation* that had gone undetected. My brain tonsils were falling into my spinal column. The neurosurgeon's words were heavy, but the message was clear—I needed brain surgery. I needed it *immediately*. While necessary, the procedure came with complications, leaving me unable to walk, talk, or work. We fought to reclaim my life for two years.

Recovery was grueling. However, what haunted me the most wasn't my own pain; it was the picture my children were left to see. I was bedridden for months, and one day, Isaiah—my sweet, perceptive boy— came home with a note from his teacher. She wanted to know how to respond to his question: "Is my mommy gonna die?"

Those five words pierced through the fog of my exhaustion and despair. They woke me up—spiritually, emotionally, and physically. I tied my limp body upright in a chair to show my children that even in weakness, I was still Mommy. I cried out to God: "You can break me, but please don't break my babies!"

The journey wasn't easy. My children faced bullying at school because of my wheelchair. They were asked hurtful questions like, "Why does your mommy have wheels and my mommy has feet?" But instead of shame, they chose courage. Together, we turned their experience into a ministry. Isaiah and Elijah co-authored, *"My Mommy Had Brain Surgery & I'm Okay"*—a book written by kids, for kids, to help other families navigate life through disability.

The book became their shield and their voice. The next time someone asked why their mommy was in a wheelchair, they proudly replied, "Buy the book—it's my college fund!" Today, that little project is so much more than a family milestone. It's a tool of hope, compassion, and understanding, used to show other children that their voices matter and even in the face of adversity, God's love can turn pain into purpose.

Finding Christ In Crisis: God Must Really Love You!

One Sunday, during a particularly low moment, I wheeled into church in a second-hand, clunky department store wheelchair. My frail body was barely upright. My spirit was weighed down by more than just my circumstances. A stranger approached me, looked me over with curious eyes, and bluntly asked, "What happened to you?"

I hesitated, unsure of how much to say, but before I could finish, he smiled and said something I'll never forget: "God must really love you." His words caught me off guard. At first, I wondered if he was mocking me, but the sincerity in his eyes told a different story. That encounter reminded me that even in brokenness, *God's love is undeniable*—and sometimes, it takes a stranger to remind us.

Life can change in an instant, and for us, it did. Without warning, our comfortable, dual-income lifestyle was swallowed by mounting medical debt. The life we had carefully built for ourselves—and our two young children—was suddenly upended.

In that season of crisis, I found Christ—not just as a savior, but as an anchor. He met me in the mess, in the moments where I thought I couldn't take one more step, and reminded me that His plans are bigger than my own. As **Isaiah 55:9** reminds us: *"As the heavens are higher than the earth, so are my ways higher than your ways and my thoughts than your thoughts."* This verse brought me comfort and reassurance that even in the most difficult moments, God's purpose for my life was far beyond what I could comprehend.

Battletested – Getting Better or Bitter

Growing up in a difficult household, I fought my way out, believing that hard work and perseverance my father taught me could overcome anything. This was just another hurdle, right? I told myself that I'd get back on my feet, reclaim my dreams, and pick up where I left off—obtaining my terminal degree. As a teenager, I put in the work to earn scholarships, but my single-parent household came with financial responsibilities. I resolved that if I ever got another chance, I'd seize it with both hands. This felt like my second chance. Surely, God wouldn't allow this detour, this devastation, to derail everything—not after I'd given my life to Him. Not as a new believer who faithfully served the church and His Kingdom. Would He?

As the weight of the crisis bore down on me, I wrestled with the tension between faith and doubt. How could this be part of His plan? Why would God allow me to lose so much—financial stability, independence, and the certainty I had built my life upon? I didn't understand it then, but looking back, I can see the quiet work He was doing in the background, even as I struggled to make sense of it all.

The truth is, sometimes God doesn't show up in the ways we expect. He strips away the things we lean on, not to punish us, but to promote us and make space for us to lean on Him. He doesn't always prevent the storm, but He stands in the middle of it, guiding us toward a greater purpose we can't see.

This wasn't just a detour. It was a *redirection*. It was a chance to learn that my worth wasn't tied to achievements or financial success but to who I am in Christ. It was in this crisis that I truly found Him—and in finding Him, I found myself. Today, I have no doubt that me and other "disabled disciples" are His favorite! He does "really love me!"

Crowns For Christ: Heavy Is The Head

It wasn't my fault. I grew up with a big brother and an awesome father who shaped my world. Don't get me wrong—I loved my mom—but while other little girls were spinning around in pink fluffy dresses, I was in the streets playing football with my brother's friends or in the garage learning how to change the oil in my dad's Cadillac.

That toughness served me well in life, especially in the male-dominated STEM field where less than 1% of the people in the room looked like me—young, Black, and female. I had grown accustomed to breaking barriers and challenging expectations, so you can imagine my reaction when someone suggested I enter a pageant for women in wheelchairs. I was offended! A pageant? Me? No thanks. I couldn't understand why anyone thought I'd be interested in competing for and wearing a crown and sash.

I learned something that completely changed my perspective. The pageant wasn't about outward beauty or position; it was about community service. Our "talent" wasn't singing or dancing—it was how we gave back to the world around us. That realization convinced and convicted me, so I gave it a shot. How could I say *no* to competing as Ms. Wheelchair Georgia if it allowed me to expand my work with children on the autism spectrum beyond my zip code?

To my surprise—and to God's glory—I won the title of Ms. Wheelchair USA for my state. Then, I went on to become the first woman of color to win the national title and the title of Ms. Wheelchair International. Suddenly, I found myself on a platform I never could have imagined, traveling the world, amplifying the voices of people with disabilities, and redefining what it means to be both beautiful and capable.

The crowns and sashes were nice, as were the international travel, sponsorships, and speaking opportunities, but what meant the most to me was the sisterhood I gained. The women I met were powerful, resilient, and inspiring. Together, we dismantled stereotypes my mother and others always conveyed, especially the one that says, "You can either be smart or pretty." Sorry, Mom, but this experience proved that you can be both— and a whole lot more.

Today, I embrace my crowns, not as symbols of vanity, but as tools for ministry, advocacy, and change. From playing football in the streets to wearing pink everything, God used my journey to show the world that strength and beauty come in all forms and that when we place our crowns at His feet, they reflect His glory.

Melanated Queens Rising: The Art Of Adaptability

In this world, how can someone be both *hypervisible* and *invisible* at the same time? It's a paradox I've lived every day—a woman of color, a leader, and a person navigating life with a disability. For women, especially Melanated queens, balancing leadership responsibilities with personal well-being and mental health isn't just challenging—it's expected. We're conditioned to wear the crown of resilience, even when it weighs us down. Yet, beneath that crown, there's a quiet truth: stress, fatigue, and feeling 'off' without quite knowing why. Millions of women in the workforce experience this, but it's often amplified for those of us who carry the dual realities of being underestimated yet overexposed.

As a leader, an advocate, and a person who intimately understands these struggles, I find myself constantly straddling the line between hypervisibility and invisibility. On one hand, I'm seen—headlines, stages, and titles—but on the other, my struggles are often dismissed or misunderstood. The irony of living the very challenges I advocate for is both humbling and heartbreaking. Yet, it's also empowering because my lived experience drives my passion to serve and creates a deeper connection with those I support.

This delicate balance is the inspiration for my book, *The Art of Adaptability: The 4/4's for Newly Disabled and Diagnosed Persons*. It's more than a guide; it's a lifeline for those grappling with the overwhelming reality of a new diagnosis or sudden disability. Each chapter unfolds like a blueprint, helping individuals rebuild their lives one day at a time. From rediscovering their identity to navigating relationships and professional spaces, the book is a reflection of my journey and a resource for anyone learning to thrive in the face of unexpected challenges. It also became a workbook for organizations to workshop with intentional inclusion.

I wrote this book not just for those experiencing disability firsthand but also for their families, caregivers, loved ones, and allies. It's a testament to the truth that being "off" doesn't mean being out of the game. It means learning and teaching new strategies, building new bridges, and most importantly, finding strength in community.

For Melanated queens rising beyond disabilities, *The Art of Adaptability* is a reminder that we don't just adapt—we *redefine* the narrative. We turn moments of invisibility into platforms of empowerment. We claim space unapologetically, balancing the weight of our crowns while adjusting crowns for others. Because while the world may see our crowns as burdens, we know they are symbols of purpose, power, and grace.

Dream, Write, And Hope – Breaking Patterns

In a moment I'll never forget, I became the first person in a wheelchair to cross the university's graduation stage in its 73-year history. As the tassel turned and the crowd cheered, I realized this wasn't just a personal milestone—it was a breakthrough for others like me. But the capstone of my journey wasn't the degree itself; it was the creation of something that would outlive my time there.

The old adage, "Necessity is the mother of invention," reminds me that establishing the university's first-ever Office of Disability Services was a labor of love born from desperation. I experienced firsthand the hurdles that neurodiverse and disabled students face—both on campus and remotely. The office became a beacon of support, providing resources, advocacy, and accommodations that many students had only dreamed of. Knowing that this foundation would serve future generations filled me with a sense of purpose and pride far greater than the honor of crossing that stage.

We drink from wells we did not dig and rest under the shade of trees we did not plant, and it is our duty to ensure others can do the same. That's why my work didn't stop at graduation. Through *Dream-Write-Hope University*, the 501(c)(3) nonprofit I founded, we continue to empower neurodivergent students with learning challenges, disabilities, and socio-economic disadvantages to pursue higher education, advocacy, and STEM careers. By providing financial scholarships and academic advocacy support, we aim to break patterns of exclusion and build inclusive legacies of literacy.

This isn't just about helping individual students; it's about lowering the ladder for those who will come after us. Every scholarship awarded, every voice amplified, every barrier dismantled—it's all part of a larger mission to create a world where access to education isn't a privilege but a right. We encourage others to contribute, share, and join us as we grow!

Faithful Resilience: Crowning A Life Worth Saving

What you won't find in my bio, CV, resume, online profiles, or even in any AI-generated report is that I am, without a doubt, the world's biggest crybaby. Yes, you read that right. I've cried more times than I can count while writing this anthology. Some of those tears were for the overwhelming gratitude I feel for God's grace—not just for the world but for me personally. I believe that all of our tears are captured in God's most priceless alabaster vessels. Nevertheless, it was as if every page of this story reminded me of how blessed I am to be alive, to share my journey, and to witness His love at work in my life.

The title of this anthology, *Crowns for Christ: A Life Worth Saving – The Yvette Pegues Story*, is not just a catchy phrase. It's the heart of my story. It represents every crown, every struggle, every triumph, and every moment of surrender to God's will. It reminds me that, despite all the twists and turns in life, God's grace has covered me every step of the way. My story is not mine alone—it's His story, too.

What I've come to realize, especially through writing this, is that answers don't always have the structure we expect and there's no such thing as a true "win" or "loss" in God's kingdom. With each perceived setback or victory, I trust that He is still on the throne, and His plans for me are far greater than I could ever imagine. And that, my friends, is why I cry. It's not out of defeat but in awe of a love so vast and a grace so abundant.

In those moments when life doesn't go as planned or the world feels too heavy, I cling to the promise in **Romans 8:28**:

"And we know that in all things, God works for the good of those who love him, who have been called according to his purpose."

This verse reminds me that no matter the circumstances, God is always working behind the scenes for our good, and nothing is wasted in His plans for us.

It is with this hope that I move forward, with unwavering and faithful resilience, remembering that my life—like all of ours—is a life worth saving. And through every crown I receive, I lay them at His feet, for they are not just mine to wear, but His to redeem. This journey isn't just about me; it's about all of *us*, walking hand in hand, as we shine a light for others to follow.

About the Author

D r. Yvette Pegues is a trailblazing advocate, author, and educator who has redefined resilience and leadership as a disabled woman of color. From her vibrant beginnings in Miami to a transformative career at IBM, her journey took an unexpected turn following a life-altering spinal cord injury. Refusing to be confined by limitations, Yvette became the first woman of color crowned Ms. Wheelchair USA, using her platform to amplify voices and break barriers.

Through her nonprofit, groundbreaking publications, and innovation in inclusive technology, Yvette's story is a testament to courage, adaptability, and a relentless pursuit of equity for marginalized communities worldwide. She is most proud of being a wife, mom, adapted sports chaplain, author, award-winning keynote/TED speaker, and global advocate for newly disabled and diagnosed persons, their families, and their care teams. In her free time, she personally participates in up to 20 different adaptive sports - from scuba diving to skydiving, surfing, golf, and more.

If you're reading this and don't fall under the medical definition of 'disabled' you, will be. In our lifetime, we are 50% more likely to experience temporary, situational, or permanent disability through accident, illness, injury, or aging. The rest of us have someone we love and care deeply for in our home, immediate family, or village. As such, remember to practice grace, offer dignity, and bless a life worth saving on your journey.

How to Connect with Yvette:

https://yvettepegues.com/
Email: info@yourinvisibledisability.com
FB: @YourInvisibleDisability
LinKedIn: yvettepegues

Acknowledgements

To my husband, my "King of David" in the storm, thank you for leading me to Christ and reminding me daily of His unwavering love and grace. You are my strength, my partner, and my steady anchor in this unexpected journey. Your faith and love have been a testament of God's divine plan, and I am eternally grateful for the role you play in my life and in our family.

To my children, you are the light that reignited my will to live, dream, and rise again after life-changing injuries. Your laughter, love, and unwavering belief in me have been a constant reminder that God's greatest blessings often look like tiny hands and boundless hearts. You inspire me to push forward every day, and you give my life immeasurable purpose.

Together, you have shown me the true meaning of love, resilience, and faith. This chapter, this story, this journey—it is all a reflection of the grace God has poured into my life through you. Thank you for being spectacular jewels in my *Crowns for Christ*.

To every **Melanated Queen Rising Beyond Disabilities** who turns these pages, this is for you. This is a testament that your story is still being written that your voice matters, and that your crown—though sometimes heavy—is a symbol of the divine strength within you. May you find hope in these words, encouragement in this journey, and the unwavering belief that you, too, are fearfully and wonderfully made. Keep rising, keep believing, and keep shining—your testimony is not just your own; it is a beacon for the world.

Phyllis Moody, Contributing Author
Author, Poet & Caregiver

From Bottles to Breakthroughs: The Power to Forgive

What is forgiveness?

To *forgive* means to pardon, forget, let go, excuse, and bear no malice. It sounds simple in theory, but in practice, forgiveness is one of the hardest things to do, especially when the pain runs deep. Forgiveness challenges us to confront our hurt, let go of resentment, and extend grace where it might not feel deserved. It is an *act of the will* that requires courage and humility, and at times, it feels like a battle within us.

Forgiveness is not about denying the hurt or pretending the pain doesn't exist. It is not a sign of weakness or surrendering to injustice. Instead, it is a conscious decision to release ourselves from the chains of anger, bitterness, and the desire for revenge. It is about choosing freedom for our hearts and souls, even when it feels undeserved.

There have been so many moments in my life where I found myself standing at the crossroads of forgiveness and bitterness, and God challenged me to take the higher road. Sometimes, that road felt impossibly steep, especially when the wounds were fresh or the offense seemed too great to overcome. The act of forgiveness often felt like I was giving something away while receiving nothing in return.

But forgiveness is not just for the other person—it is for *us*, too. It allows us to heal, to move forward, and to live without the burden of past hurts weighing us down. It's about trusting God to deal with the justice while we embrace the peace that only He can provide.

Colossians 3:13 (ESV) says, *"Bearing with one another, if one has a complaint against another, forgiving each other, as the Lord has forgiven you, so you must forgive."* Those words have echoed in my heart countless times. But I've often found myself asking, "Why is it always me? Why am I the one who has to be the bigger person?"

Forgiveness can feel unfair and lonely, like we are carrying the weight of making things right while others continue without remorse. But in those moments, I've learned to lean on God's strength, to remember how much I have been forgiven, and to trust that His plans are greater than my understanding.

This is where my story begins—the moments when forgiveness didn't feel like an option but became a necessity for my own peace and healing. Let me share how God worked in my heart, even when it felt impossible.

When I was growing up in a beautiful, small, historic town in the Low Country, life seemed carefree and simple. Nestled between moss-draped oaks and winding marshes, the world around me felt like a postcard come to life. My childhood was filled with the laughter of playing outdoors, the freedom of running barefoot on sun-warmed dirt roads, and the quiet hum of cicadas in the evening air. To anyone looking in, my life would have seemed idyllic, a picture of innocence and possibility.

As a child, I enjoyed the simplicity of youth, exploring my surroundings with wide-eyed curiosity. I had an adventurous spirit, always eager to climb the tallest tree or catch the fleeting shimmer of dragonflies by the water's edge. I was outgoing and friendly, but there was also a quiet side to me—a part that found solace in solitude, drawing pictures in the sand or losing myself in the pages of a favorite book. I was the kind of child who would light up a room but never demand attention. That quiet nature, I believe, made me both approachable and tragically, an easy target.

There's a particular kind of trust children have in the adults around them. We look up to them as protectors, as people who will guide us and keep us safe. But what happens when the very person meant to shield you from harm becomes the source of it?

One of my male relatives crossed boundaries that should never be crossed. He was someone I trusted, someone who was supposed to look out for me. At the time, I couldn't fully grasp the gravity of his actions. My young mind struggled to understand why he acted the way he did, and in my confusion, I sometimes wondered if he was carrying wounds of his own—pains and struggles that no one had ever helped him confront.

But understanding him—or trying to—didn't erase the harm he caused me. His actions planted seeds of confusion and shame in my heart, seeds that grew and tangled around my sense of self-worth for years to come. I didn't have the words to articulate my feelings back then. I just knew something about it felt deeply *wrong*, yet I was too afraid to say anything. The fear was overwhelming—fear of being blamed, fear of not being believed, fear of shattering the fragile image of family harmony.

It's strange how childhood innocence can coexist with a burden so heavy. I would go from playing outside and laughing with friends to moments of silent anguish, carrying a secret I didn't even fully understand. There were days I felt invisible; my voice swallowed by the enormity of what I was enduring. The betrayal was like a shadow, following me even when I tried to step into the light.

Looking back now, I can see how those experiences shaped me—not just the pain they caused but the resilience they demanded. I had to learn, far too young, how to carry hurt without letting it define me. The journey to forgiveness, to healing, would be long and filled with twists and turns. But even then, in the depths of my pain, there was a flicker of hope, a whisper that someday I would find my way out of the darkness.

I was only ten years old when an incident changed my perspective on life. I had just stepped out of the bathroom, and in that moment, I felt a deep sense of confusion and fear. He said hurtful things and acted in ways that made me uncomfortable. As a child, I didn't have the words to explain what was wrong, but I instinctively knew it wasn't right.

He used manipulation to keep me silent, telling me no one would believe me and that I was powerless to stop him. At that age, I didn't know how to navigate those emotions or where to turn for help. The experience left me feeling small and unsure of myself, and I withdrew into a quieter version of who I once was.

The Silence That Hurts

One day, while my grandmother was sweeping the porch, she noticed me sitting on his lap. Her reaction was immediate, and I was told to go to the upper part of the house until my parents returned home. I didn't fully understand what was happening, but I knew from her expression that something was wrong.

When my mother was informed of the situation, I hoped that she would protect me, confront him, and make sense of the confusing emotions I was experiencing. Instead, I was met with a whipping. In that moment, I was made to feel as though *I* was the one at fault, as though I had done something wrong. No further conversations were had, no explanations were given, and the incident was swept under the rug, never to be spoken of again.

In many Black families and churches, there is an unspoken rule to address difficult situations with silence or prayer rather than confrontation and accountability. It's a legacy rooted in resilience—one that taught our ancestors how to survive unimaginable oppression—but it often leaves those who are hurting without a voice or the support they need to heal. The mantra of "what happens in this house, stays in this house" perpetuates a cycle of secrecy, where wounds fester beneath the surface, unseen and untreated.

For me, this approach created years of internal conflict. I questioned my worth daily, wondering if I was somehow to blame for the things that had happened to me. I carried a burden that wasn't mine to bear, and the weight of it seeped into every corner of my life. The pain was always there, simmering beneath a carefully constructed exterior, threatening to boil over when no one was watching.

I didn't know how to cope with the emotional scars I carried, so I sought escape wherever I could find it. For me, that escape came in the form of alcohol. At first, it dulled the pain, quieted the chaos in my mind, and made me feel like I could breathe again. But what started as a coping mechanism quickly became a crutch. I began drinking more and more, convincing myself that I had it under control, even as my life spiraled out of it.

My decisions during that time were clouded by the haze of my addiction. I found myself in and out of jail, tangled in situations I never imagined for myself. It seemed like every time I tried to climb out of the hole I was in, something would pull me back down. I sought validation in all the wrong places, meeting men who mirrored the dysfunction I had experienced growing up. They offered temporary affection, but their love came with conditions, manipulation, and at times, even more pain. I didn't believe I deserved better because I didn't think I was better.

My days became a blur of regret and self-destruction. The same girl who once ran barefoot through the marshes and dreamed of the stars was now lost, a shadow of herself. I wanted to stop the cycle, to turn things around, but I didn't know how. Shame whispered that I was too far gone, that I had messed up too much to deserve a second chance.

It wasn't until I hit rock bottom—facing the harsh reality of what my life had become—that I realized something had to change. The silence that had been imposed on me as a child no longer served me. I couldn't keep sweeping my pain under the rug, hoping it would disappear. I had to confront it head-on, even if that meant tearing down walls I'd spent years building.

It was in those moments, broken and desperate, that I began to seek true healing. Not the kind of healing that came from numbing the pain, but the kind that came from addressing it, owning it, and deciding to rise above it.

Looking back, I recognize the cultural and generational challenges that contributed to this response. Conversations around abuse, mental health, and trauma were often avoided, as they were seen as too painful or too taboo to address openly. But avoiding the conversation doesn't erase the pain—it prolongs it.

The Power of Letting Go

My father was a military man, and when we were stationed in Havelock, North Carolina, away from that particular family member, the abuse stopped. However, the damage had already been done. I began acting out, a clear sign of the turmoil I was experiencing. My mother noticed the changes in my behavior, but instead of addressing the root cause, she often met me with words that left me feeling even more isolated. She would say there was nothing she could do about it now and encouraged me to read Psalm 121 with her repeatedly.

At the time, I refused. I felt so unworthy, so tainted, that I believed touching the Bible would cause it to burn. I had internalized the idea that what happened to me was my fault, and when I was met with physical punishment instead of compassion, it only reinforced those feelings of guilt and shame.

As I grew older, I made a conscious decision to distance myself from that family member entirely. I never spoke to him again and made it a priority to ensure that none of my daughters were ever left alone with him. Protecting them became my way of reclaiming the power I felt I had lost during my own childhood.

Eight years ago, I received a call from another family member informing me that the relative who had hurt me was gravely ill with cancer. I initially felt nothing but indifference and told them I had nothing to say. However, out of respect and love for the family member who called, I decided to reach out. The conversation was brief. He apologized to me for the pain he had caused so many years ago.

In that moment, I told him I had forgiven him—not for his sake but for mine. Forgiveness was a gift I gave to myself, a way to release the lingering anger and hurt that had weighed me down for so long. It brought me an unexpected sense of peace and divine freedom. That conversation marked the beginning of a journey—a journey toward healing, grace, and a deeper understanding of what it truly means to forgive.

I've endured things that left scars—situations that shaped me in ways I didn't always recognize until much later. Pain that I carried silently, mistakes I made in response to that pain, and regrets I wish I could erase. Life has a way of throwing us into situations where forgiveness feels almost impossible, where the weight of what someone has done to us feels too heavy to let go.

But holding on to anger, resentment, and pain only weighs me down. It's like drinking poison and expecting the other person to suffer. I've learned that forgiveness isn't about excusing what happened or pretending it didn't hurt—it's about freeing myself from the chains of bitterness. It's about making peace with my past and trusting God to handle the justice part.

Forgiveness doesn't mean forgetting. I remember everything. But it does mean I can face those memories without allowing them to control me. It means I can let God use my pain to grow me, to strengthen me, and even to help others. Forgiving doesn't make me weak; it makes me stronger because it means I've chosen to rise above what tried to break me.

Each time I've chosen to forgive, I've felt a little lighter. It's not easy, and sometimes it feels like a daily decision, but I know it's worth it. God forgave me—flaws, mistakes, and all. How can I not strive to extend that same grace to others?

As I grew older, I came to understand that what happened wasn't my fault. The blame didn't belong to me, and I refused to carry the weight of shame he tried to place on my shoulders. A sense of empowerment replaced the fear that once controlled me.

Echoes of the Past: Going back in time

When I was a younger, a family member and his brothers were at my home while I was outside in the yard, playing with a doll my father had sent me from Japan. Out of nowhere, that family member hesitantly told me that the man I called my father wasn't my biological dad. He revealed the identity of my real father and told me he lived in Pennsylvania.

Hearing that my beloved father wasn't biologically mine sent a chill down my spine. I loved him deeply, but I needed to know the truth. That summer, at the age of 17, I decided to fly to Philadelphia to meet my biological father and my other siblings.

Not long after reconnecting with my new family, another family member did things to me that were inappropriate—similar to what a different family member had done before. I asked him, "Why are you doing this to me?"

He responded, "I just don't want you to get pregnant." I couldn't comprehend why someone I trusted would hurt me this way.

When I told my grandmother about what had happened, she dismissed it, saying, "He wouldn't do that—he's family." Another relative told me it would be better if I never said anything. My sister, however, confided in me that the same man would get drunk and say things to her that were inappropriate as well.

What do you do when the people you trust continue to betray you? I couldn't stay. I decided to leave and vowed never to return. But I did come back—because of my sister. I loved her and wanted to protect her.

During those visits, I tried to fit in for the sake of my siblings. I attended block parties, cookouts, and other family gatherings, even though it pained me. My siblings told me I needed to forgive him, but they didn't understand how much I was suffering. I forced smiles, drunk alcohol continuously, and it became my escape.

Despite everything, I still carried the weight of what he did to me. Then, at the age of 46, after years of suppressing my pain, I got drunk and picked up the phone. I called that family member and said, "I've waited my whole life to tell you this. You know what you did to me—but I forgive you."

He tried to admit some vague apology, claiming he had told me he was sorry before, but I knew it wasn't true. He was gaslighting me. If he had truly cared about me, maybe my life would have been different. I wouldn't have carried the burden of being taken advantage of or turned to alcohol whenever I felt depressed or unwanted. His actions shaped so much of my pain, and I often wondered what my life could have been if he hadn't hurt me.

A few years later, that family member passed away due to health issues. The night before he died, he asked my sister to contact me. She didn't tell me until the day he passed. I felt cheated, like she had taken away my chance to hear what he wanted to say face to face. But instead of letting resentment take over, I chose forgiveness. My faith in God wouldn't allow me to stop speaking to my sister over it.

Forgiveness is powerful. It didn't erase the pain, but it gave me the strength to move forward. Even though the scars remain, I refuse to let them define me.

Rising from the Ashes

In 2010, I was still living in Philadelphia. I had owned my home since 2000 and had been working at the hospital since 1999. One day, while on Facebook, I reconnected with an old love, a veteran I had known since 1981. We started talking every day, and I made the mistake of moving him from Ohio to Philadelphia.

The night he stepped off the Greyhound bus, I could see that life had not been kind to him. He was only about 180 pounds, a shadow of the man I once knew. My sister was with me at the bus station, and she looked at me and asked, "What are you going to do?"

Months after taking him in and caring for him, I got him back to looking like the fine black Marine I once remembered—he gained weight, reaching 215 pounds. But I must have given him too much confidence because that's when the real nightmare began.

He became violent. He started fighting me, giving me black eyes, busted lips, and fractures. He shoved my head into brick walls and dragged me up three flights of stairs. I lied to the ER staff and my coworkers, trying to protect him. By the time it was over, I had gone from owning a five-bedroom single home to living in a rented, roach-and-mouse-infested one-bedroom apartment.

He once told me, "You made me feel like the phoenix that rose out of the ashes." But behind that façade, I discovered he was still married. I thought he was betraying me, but I realized he had been lying to me all along.

The pain and guilt consumed me. I started drinking heavily and ended up with a DUI and a simple assault charge. But nothing broke me more than learning what he had done to my 12-year-old granddaughter. She didn't tell me until she was 15, after her mother found her suicide note and questioned her. That was when she revealed everything. I was devastated, drowning in guilt and shame, blaming myself for ever bringing him into our lives.

I wanted to kill him, but deep down, I knew he wasn't worth losing my life over. So, I bought him a one-way ticket back to Akron and sent him away for good.

It was my granddaughter—just 16 at the time—who taught me the true power of forgiveness. Her words still echo in my heart: "He wounded me, Grandma, but he didn't ruin me, and I forgive him."

Her strength moved me. If she could find it in her heart to forgive him, why couldn't I? Today, she's a 19-year-old college student, pursuing her dreams of becoming a journalist and photographer. She hopes to one day attend Temple University, and I couldn't be prouder of her resilience and courage.

Over the years, I've faced so many situations that forced me to learn the value of forgiveness. I've learned to forgive because I've been forgiven. Forgiveness is one of the greatest gifts God has given us, and I now understand that forgiving is not for the other person—it's for yourself.

Conclusion:
A Journey to Forgiveness and Self-Love

Today, I stand as a testament to the power of forgiveness, resilience, and God's grace. I am a mother, grandmother, author, and caretaker—a woman who has endured the storms of life but found strength and healing in her faith. My journey has not been an easy one, but every challenge I faced has shaped me into the person I am today.

There was a time when alcohol was my escape, my way of numbing the pain and guilt that weighed so heavily on my soul. I was trapped in a cycle of self-destruction, carrying the burdens of my past and blaming myself for things I could not control. But one day, I looked in the mirror and realized I didn't recognize the woman staring back at me. I knew I deserved more.

I turned to God, seeking His guidance and love, and slowly, I began to rebuild my life. I learned to forgive—not just those who had hurt me but also myself. I forgave the woman who once doubted her worth, the mother who thought she had failed, and the granddaughter who carried guilt that was never hers to bear.

Through this process, I discovered the beauty of loving myself. I realized that forgiveness is not about excusing the actions of others but about freeing yourself from the chains of anger and resentment. Forgiveness gave me peace, and that peace allowed me to fully embrace my purpose.

Today, I live with a heart full of gratitude. I am blessed to be a mother to amazing children who have taught me so much about strength and unconditional love. I am a proud grandmother to a young woman whose resilience inspires me every day. I am an author, sharing my story and my truth in the hopes that it will help others find their own path to healing.

As a caretaker, I now dedicate my life to serving and uplifting others. Whether it's providing care to loved ones or offering a listening ear to someone in need, I find joy in being a source of support and compassion.

Most importantly, I am a woman who loves herself and her God. I wake up each day with a renewed sense of purpose and faith, knowing that my journey is far from over. I am not defined by the struggles of my past but by the strength and love that carried me through them.

To anyone reading this who may be struggling with their own pain, I want you to know that *forgiveness* is possible. *Healing* is possible. You are more than your scars, more than your mistakes, and more than the hardships you've endured. Love yourself, trust in God, and allow forgiveness to set you free.

This is not the end of my story—it's just the beginning of a new chapter, one filled with hope, love, and endless possibilities.

Look in the Mirror

Look in the mirror, now can I tell you what I truly see?
She is no longer a stranger, for she is really me.

No longer do I have to run and hide,
No longer do I shame the tears I cry.

For there is no more room for the negative things,
I used to hold deep within my heart's strings.
Yes, those things no longer play in my life a key part,
I looked up and at myself, decided to take a peek,
There is strength now where I used to be so weak.

There was no hope I found down in the beer can,
But if I came along with self-worth,

Grab and hold of my trembling hands.
I don't need to lay down and give myself to a man,
That means me no good, God has a plan.

For me, and He wouldn't give up until these things I understand.
So yes, when I look in the mirror, I see,
Her reflection looking back at me, and she smiles now, because we both
have finally been set free.

About the Author

Phyllis is a gifted poet, author, and dedicated caregiver who has touched many lives through her words and actions. With a passion for storytelling, she weaves emotions and experiences into poetry that resonates deeply with her readers. As a mother and grandmother, Phyllis cherishes the bonds she shares with her family, offering wisdom and love through every chapter of her life.

Beyond her literary accomplishments, she is a compassionate caregiver, providing unwavering support to those in need. Her work is a reflection of her resilience, kindness, and commitment to making the world a better place, one word and one act of kindness at a time. Phyllis's journey is one of strength, love, and a deep connection to her community.

How to Connect with Phyllis:

Email: mspjmoody@gmail.com
FB: @Phyllis Moody
Instagram: @phyllis.moody.509

Acknowledgments

To Yahweh, these are Your words, Lord, and not my own. I humbly ask that You continue to use me as a vessel, guiding me to speak truth to Your sheep and to share the messages You have entrusted to me. May I always serve Your purpose and lead others closer to You through the words You place in my heart.

To my parents, your steadfast love and unwavering support have been the foundation of my strength. No matter the circumstances, you have stood by me with grace and unconditional love, and for that, I am eternally grateful.

To my beautiful daughters, you are the greatest blessing the Lord has ever bestowed upon me. Your presence fills my heart with immeasurable joy and gratitude. Being your parent is the highest honor, and I thank God daily for the privilege of walking this journey with you.

To my grandchildren, the precious lights of my life, you are the jewels in my crown. Your innocence, laughter, and unconditional love brighten even my darkest days.

To the many men and women who have suffered from abuse, this story is dedicated to you. I see your strength, your resilience, and your courage. I pray that you find healing, peace, and the power to forgive—not for those who have hurt you, but for your own freedom and well-being. If you are struggling with addiction as a result of trauma, I encourage you to seek help. The National Helpline for Substance Abuse and Mental Health Services is available 24/7 at 1-800-662-HELP (4357).

A heartfelt thank you to *Welcome To The Storm Publishing* for your unwavering dedication and support throughout this journey. Your commitment to excellence and your belief in my vision have made this story possible. Thank you for helping me share my story with the world.

Krystal Monteros, Contributing Author

Ms. Wheelchair Washington, 2010
State Coordinator, Ms. Wheelchair Washington
Co-Founder, EMWA (Empowerment Movement of Washington State)

The Strength in Struggle:

Embracing Life's Challenges with Faith and Determination!

If we have the strength to keep our eyes open, we move further every second of that time. Living with limited conditions brings an increased number of struggles. We are not as close to the average person as we may seem. Many aspects of our lives are overlooked. This only means that our lives carry even more meaning because, whether we realize it or not, we are constantly working and striving toward goals that are not evident to the average eye. If we bail out on even one goal or dream, we are bailing out on the life we know.

All of our unbeatable struggles bring us face-to-face with every possible type of depression. This draws us closer to God because, for the majority of the time, the only comfort we have is shown to us through His love. His love is the one thing we will never lose. God's love allows us to sleep peacefully because we know He has everything under His wings. He understands the reason for even the most microscopic event needing to take place. Every day, He brings new challenges, whether we ask for them or not. We are forced to quickly and quietly develop some form of strength and a way of enduring the many things most often frowned upon by the average person.

Whether seen or not, these obstacles and challenges create struggles that, in turn, give us an advantage over others. This is because the hardest of times shine a light on more reasons to appreciate the place we stand in life. They help us credit ourselves for every success we achieve. Whether the step is big or small, it is still success in our journey toward finishing the greatest maze. We learn that without struggle, there is no progress. If we are not forced to navigate the blocks and bumps in our path, how can we conclude that there's nothing we cannot overcome?

No matter how hard life gets, our attitude and outlook on our situations are the keys to determining how far we can go. We see more and more of our success and how far we've come as the years, months, and even days pass. If we don't live life to its fullest, how can we inspire anyone else to do the same? We learn to take advantage of the things we have because we understand that those things may not always be available and can easily be lost if we don't keep our goals, determination, and dreams alive. As long as those three things keep moving and growing, we keep living. The minute any one of them is stolen or begins to slightly decline, our souls begin to lose their vitality.

With all this comes an appreciation for the things not yet found and a strong way of cherishing the unbreakable blessings we have experienced. At the lowest times in our lives, we often have little to no motivation. If we don't want to go on for ourselves, our only motivation is to keep going for those around us. By continuing for just one more day, we may be helping them in ways we cannot see.

We are unlike any other. As we move forward to conquer our dreams and goals, the people we once thought were most compatible with us may no longer understand how different things truly are. They fail to grasp that while we may need help opening doors, we also need the chance to open those doors ourselves the next time. Though people might think they understand our situation based on appearances, they never truly will. Imagine wanting and fighting to blend in while knowing deep down that it will never happen.

The moments that leave the greatest impact are those of struggle, pain, confusion, strength, revelation, and conquering. All these experiences take place deep within our soul. These moments cannot be shared with just anyone; only a rare few are privileged and special enough to gain access to that sacred place within us. Very few people can comprehend the depth and complexity of the feelings, thoughts, and emotions tied to the numerous limitations we face daily. Finding that one person who truly understands would be an extraordinary blessing.

We see, live, and learn from everything in a different, more precious way than those who fail to acknowledge how much they have always had and how truly blessed they are. We've always heard the saying, "Many are called, but few are chosen." We were the chosen ones to take on the heroic mission of living with various limitations. God saw something unique and special in us, showing Him that we, above all others, were capable of enduring, growing, and inspiring change through our lives. For this reason, we are honored to be among God's chosen. We have the potential to make an enormous difference with every experience we encounter, even in ways we may never fully understand.

It is rare for someone to say with pride that they are glad to live a life unlike any other. Will we ever find someone who truly understands everything it takes to keep going with limitations? What it takes to strive for the next level without knowing what that level is, when it will come, how it will arrive, who will be involved, what it will lead to, or why it must happen?

It's hard to imagine if there is even one person who feels you are important enough to devote themselves to a relationship where the ultimate goal is recognizing that as long as you are at peace with yourself, you can find peace with everything the world brings your way. Will anyone ever truly understand the immense baggage that comes from having even one single visible limitation? Will anyone make me laugh when I want to cry?

Through the Fire: A Journey of Strength and Survival

Is there someone out there who will honor me by being the person I seek? Will there ever be someone who can bring any form of comfort to a permanently twisted mind and heart?

I wrote these words when I was just 19 years old, during my time in college. I was already struggling to earn my Associate Degree. Many looked at me and assumed that as long as my physical accommodations were met, I'd be fine. Little did they know about the emotional weight I was carrying inside, creating countless obstacles. Years of ignoring the mental torment—both inflicted by others and myself—had taken a toll. I finally poured it all out in writing because I couldn't hold it in anymore.

I had decided that bulimia did not belong to me. I became bulimic around the age of 14. I was born with Spina Bifida, paralyzed from just above my knees down. From birth to eight months old, I endured about 30 surgeries to address Spina Bifida, Clubbed Feet, and Hydrocephalus.

When I was 9 years old, doctors discovered I had Scoliosis. My spine was curving severely toward my heart, and they wanted to perform surgery immediately to correct it with rods. This was just before Christmas in 1995. My mom insisted the surgery be postponed until after the holidays so I could enjoy the time with my family. I went in for surgery on January 2, 1996. I remember that day vividly. No one could have predicted the impact it would have on my life.

We arrived at the hospital so early in the morning that it was still dark outside. Wrapped in my dad's arms, snuggled in a blanket, I waited. Hospitals were familiar to me. In my mind, I was simply following what my mom wanted me to do. I didn't think much about what was actually about to happen.

Unfortunately, the surgery led to complications. An infection developed after the procedure, and the rods had to be removed to prevent it from spreading. It turned out the infection had reached my shunt, which drained excess fluid from my brain caused by Hydrocephalus. The shunt was connected to my heart at the time, so it had to be removed immediately to prevent the infection from spreading further.

To address the fluid buildup, the doctors redirected the drainage externally. For weeks, they came into my hospital room multiple times a day to flush the shunt and administer antibiotics to fight the infection. This remains one of the most traumatizing medical experiences of my life. I was only nine years old. I still vividly remember a nurse saying, "Okay, get ready. You're about to feel something cold going through your head," while the doctor prepared the procedure. To this day, anything involving my head during medical care makes me freeze.

Eventually, the shunt was replaced, but the ordeal didn't end there. The rods were removed and replaced multiple times. I underwent two skin grafts and endured 99 Hyperbaric Oxygen treatments. Six months passed, and the physical and emotional scars deepened. I learned that I had developed trauma around anything involving my head, IVs, or skin grafts.

Although time has passed, and medical procedures have evolved over the last twenty years, the mere mention of IVs or skin grafts brings me back to those moments. The flashbacks are vivid, as if it all happened yesterday.

Silent Struggles and a Mother's Love

During high school, everything began to go downhill for me. I started to realize that the exclusion, teasing, and stares weren't because of who I was but because of my disability. I was "different." I thought long and hard about how I could change this situation, but I came up with nothing. This marked the start of my depression. I stayed up all night thinking about why I wasn't as happy as my twin. I wanted to be as pretty as her. I wanted to be as popular as her. I wanted to be the one invited to the party—not just the sister of the girl who was invited to the party. I really began to feel jealous of her.

Because I kept everything bottled inside, the pain and loneliness built up deeper and deeper. I tried to talk about it with my family, but they either ignored me or told me to calm down, saying I was overreacting or being too emotional. To release the pain, I escalated from starving myself to bulimia. Everything that went into my system came back out. I didn't want any emotions to stay within me. Bulimia became my way of release.

Since I couldn't figure out a solution to my problems, I began to believe the only way out was to end my life. Without realizing it, I started starving myself. I drank fruit juices instead of eating meals. I ate tiny dinners so my family would think I had eaten. I thought about ways to end my life, but thanks to God, I always encountered obstacles that prevented me from going through with it. As time went on, my depression deepened. After graduating high school, I wanted to change my mindset and be genuinely happy, but I still couldn't see it as a reality.

When I was 27 years old, my mom became very sick. I was the one responsible for taking care of her. Before I was born, she had been hit by a van, and that accident had damaged her equilibrium, causing balance problems. That was all I had ever known about her. As she became sicker, she began to fall more often. I had to care for her more and more. It got to the point where she shattered her elbow and broke a rib in the same fall. Witnessing her endure all these medical problems while caring for her through them brought back so many memories of my own struggles.

My mom had a bone infection in her elbow at the same time I had a bone infection in my toe. Doctors wanted to amputate her arm, just as doctors wanted to amputate my foot. I had a central line in my neck pumping antibiotics daily, praying it would heal the bone infection. Meanwhile, she had a PICC line in her arm that I administered antibiotics through daily so she could keep her arm. I had previously developed a blood clot from a PICC line, which was why I now had a central line. Yet, here I was, caring for my mom's PICC line.

One morning at 4 a.m., while she had the PICC line, my mom woke up in a disoriented state and tried to walk and move on her own. By this point, she was supposed to use a walker for support. I immediately blocked her in the bathroom so she couldn't go anywhere and called my sister, telling her something was wrong. She arrived within minutes and took my mom to the emergency room. It turned out that my mom's protein levels had dropped, and she was hallucinating. At this point, her arm was somehow connected to her stomach—I don't remember why. In this hallucinatory state, she tore the skin apart, requiring a skin graft.

Hearing the words "skin graft" was something I hadn't expected. I was still processing the fact that I had just prevented my mom from hurting herself, even as I lay paralyzed on the floor, while she wandered around hallucinating and pulling the sliding door off the closet. Now, a skin graft? My sister kept reassuring me that medical technology had advanced, but I had to summon immediate mental strength to cope. Not for me—this was for my mom.

My mom kept fighting. The day I called the ambulance to take her to the hospital, she was hallucinating. I just knew things weren't right anymore. Even in her hallucinated state, a precious moment occurred before the EMTs arrived. It was just the two of us in the apartment. Throughout my journey of searching for myself and independence as a young adult with a disability, we had a history of arguing and fighting. But in that moment of uncertainty, she looked at me and said, "Thank you for loving me so much to take care of me. I am your mom. I'm supposed to take care of you. I love you."

The fact that she acknowledged my efforts, even in her fragile state, erased all the past resentment I had felt toward her. That moment meant the world to me. As a kid, all I ever wanted was to feel heard. My mom finally took the time to recognize my care and love. I will never forget that moment.

One week later, on March 7, 2013, my mom went to Heaven.

Unbreakable: The Battle Within

I am in this battle. I don't know what to do. All I can do is stand. I can't fall. I can't go back. I have no choice. My life is not my own. At the same time, this battle brings so much confusion. Why? No one knows the battles I face—the endless questions. I have no choice but to trust in MY God. He is all I have. I'm in battle mode. So many don't even know the beginning of what I face every day.

I've conquered these battles in my mind, yet the enemy keeps reminding me of what MY God has already washed away. This is a constant beatdown that I battle unexpectedly. It strikes at the most random times—right when I make up my mind to increase my goals, praise, prayer, worship, work, ministry, and action. That is when it strikes the hardest.

I understand my life has a purpose. I understand I have a calling from the most high. That doesn't mean it's easy. This makes me fight even harder. This is a constant battle, but at the same time, it's the greatest blessing. It doesn't make sense, but I am honored that the enemy chooses to bring these battles my way. It shows that he views me as a threat.

All these mind-twisting thoughts are doing nothing but making me stronger and even more unbreakable. I am the daughter of the Most High. Keep messing with me—MY God will always place me on top.

Where would I be without my struggle? Where would I be without my pain? I may be on the bus, but I still have favor because favor is not what

I have; it's who has me. My disability does not define me. MY God is who defines me. I am the daughter of the Highest. He chose me to bring honor and glory to Him through the obstacles and victories that having a disability brings. I count it a privilege to be crowned with that honor.

Even though I was nervous, I applied for the position—and I got accepted! I served nine years on the city's Commission on Disabilities. Four of those years, I served as President. After spending so many years of life feeling unheard, God placed me in a position to make change in my community for people in my position. I was the voice being heard by those in charge.

So much change was made in my city! Sidewalks were placed in redlined areas, bus routes were changed, and closed captioning bills were passed.

God told me: Claim what is yours. Don't be afraid to say no to the battles with your emotions and mind. Finish strong. Go into 2016 flying, not dragging. Believe you will see nothing but greatness. Think it daily. Speak it daily. Privately declare, "I will see nothing but greatness everywhere I go this week." Have expectation in your heart and keep your head up.

Rising Above: Embracing Strength Through Struggle

In 2016, I was forced to move from the apartment complex where I had lived for 10 years. I had lived there with my mom, and after she passed away, I was forced to move into a one-bedroom unit. I didn't want to get used to an entirely new living environment as an independent person living with a disability, so I simply transferred to another unit within the same complex. Now, however, they were raising the rent, and I could no longer afford it.

I looked everywhere for a new place! Eventually, I moved in with my twin sister while I searched for a new apartment. Keep in mind, her place wasn't wheelchair accessible. This really challenged my mental health and independence. I couldn't even go outside the door unless she was home from work. Meanwhile, in order to confidently determine whether an apartment would work for me, I had to be able to look at it myself. I stayed there for eight months, and during that time, as difficult as it was, I kept going back to the apartments where I had previously lived. I knew they were accessible. The only problem was that I used to live there with my mom. Every time I got off the bus to go to the office for an update on availability, memories and flashbacks started to come back. I found out they only had two-bedroom accessible units available, so I settled for one of those. It was the exact same floor plan as the unit I had lived in with my mom. The mind games continued.

I had lived alone in my previous unit, but in this one, I chose to have a roommate simply to help keep my mind under control. When I lived with my mom, she had the master bedroom. I couldn't handle taking that room, so I let my roommate have it. It took so much strength just to continue waking up daily, but I did it—for my mom. As hard as it was, I held on to the word that MY God had given me for the year.

Not only did moving back into this unit remind me of my mom, but it also brought back memories of my best friend, Tony. It was in those apartments that he and I teamed up to show my mom just how independent I could be as a young adult woman who uses a wheelchair. Everything I did independently brought back so many memories. I also had to now show others, aside from my mom, that I was able to live on my own as a twenty-seven-year-old adult.

While serving on the Commission on Disabilities, I became a victim of domestic violence. Aside from the natural trauma that came from the situation, the leader MY God had formed me into was not pleased with how the police handled the situation. I fought with the Commission on Disabilities to address this, and I eventually secured a face-to-face meeting with the Police Chief. It was there that I was offered my first paid position. I chose to rise above everything I had gone through. I faced those who had wronged me, and now I am a trainer on Ableism. My first Ableism presentation was with the Fire Department in my city. With each presentation, I get to teach from my lived experience and share my stories to make change in my community.

Through all the struggles, I have learned that a woman is strong when she observes self-respect, self-esteem, and self-worth. Sometimes, we need to cover the one whom we don't want to pray for. Then, your head shall be lifted above your enemy. Work unto the Lord, not unto any person. Do what you have to do and go after what you have prayed for. In my case, it was to get justice for women with disabilities in communities that are often overlooked. Always return to why God placed you in that situation with the order to pray, and He will promote you.

He has not allowed my enemies to get the victory over me. Even though I am always messing up, MY God will never stay angry with me. His mercy is everlasting, and His grace is sufficient. Even when I fall short, He still sees the best in me. He loves me so much that I just have to learn how to get into His presence—because in His presence, there is peace, healing, and restoration. I want to show others the same love He has shown me—the love that surpasses all understanding.

Thank You, God, for not just being God, but for being MY God. When the weight of the world is on my shoulders, You remind me that I don't have to carry it alone. Because I know I can rest in You, I continue to learn how to give myself away and trust You completely. Even in my weakest moments, You remain strong for me. Even when I question my own worth, You remind me that I am fearfully and wonderfully made.

Through it all, the biggest lesson I have learned is that **being happy doesn't mean everything is perfect—it means you've decided to see beyond the imperfections.** Happiness is a choice, a mindset, and a declaration that no matter what life throws my way, I will not be defeated. Every scar, every trial, every setback has only made me stronger.

Just because people have disabilities doesn't mean that we have limits. **Our abilities are not defined by what the world sees as limitations.** We are visionaries, creators, innovators, and leaders. Together, we are stronger when we empower, encourage, and support one another. **Limitations should not be an obstacle but rather an opportunity to rise above expectations.** We all face challenges in life, but it is how we choose to confront those challenges that defines who we are.

I am not perfect, but I am pressing forward, step by step, faith by faith, until I reach the finish line. **I will keep moving, keep growing, keep believing—because my journey is not over yet.** I refuse to give up, and I refuse to settle. No matter how many times I stumble, I will rise again.

To anyone reading this, know that **your story is not over either.** You are stronger than you think, braver than you know, and more powerful than you can imagine. Keep going. Keep believing. Keep fighting for your dreams. **You were created for a purpose, and your purpose is greater than any challenge you face.**

I am not perfect, but I'm going until I make it to the end—and I hope you will too.

About the Author

Krystal Monteros is a dedicated community advocate with over a decade of experience in driving social change. Born and raised in Southern California, she now resides in Tacoma, Washington. Krystal holds an associate degree in Sociology and has been actively serving her community since 2010 through leadership roles on various boards and committees.

Her work focuses on supporting individuals with disabilities, addressing homelessness, and empowering youth. Krystal's ability to transform personal challenges into opportunities for growth has fueled her passion for creating meaningful and lasting impact.

With a strong commitment to fostering inclusivity and resilience, Krystal continues to dedicate her time and expertise to building stronger communities and improving the lives of others.

How to Connect with Krystal:

Email: babykeitho@aol.com
FB: @Krystal Monteros
Instagram: @krystal_monteros
LinKedIn: Krystal Monteros

Acknowledgements

Special thanks to my incredible family and friends, whose unwavering support, encouragement, and belief in me have been invaluable throughout this journey. I am deeply grateful for each of you who stood by my side, providing love, strength, and inspiration.

To the exceptional individuals whose hard work, dedication, and expertise brought this project to life, I extend my heartfelt appreciation. Your tireless efforts and commitment to excellence have been instrumental in shaping this endeavor, and I am truly blessed to have had such a talented and devoted team working alongside me. Thank you for being a part of this milestone.

Shakethia Shaw, Contributing Author

Accountant

Disability Advocate

*Student Association -Disability
Awareness Chair-2003*

*Oxford Mayor's Awareness Committee on Disability Issues
(2004-2007)*

Rising Above the Concrete: A Journey of Love, Loss, and Faith

Good Friday-April 14, 1995

I grew up in a two-parent home with an older sister and brother. I was a tomboy, climbing trees, learning how to cut grass, and playing outside. I was definitely a daddy's girl—wherever he went, I wanted to be right by his side. As a child, I struggled with being overweight, which led to some insecurities. My sister was the pretty one, and in my mind, I was the cute, fat sister.

I remember my sister and I joking about having a half-brother, but my mom would stop us and say, "There's no such thing as a half; you have a BROTHER." She always treated my brother as if he was her own, even when he periodically stayed with us. My mom was loving but also straightforward—a tell-it-like-it-is kind of woman. Sometimes, she embarrassed us in restaurants and stores. If the server was rude, she got rude right back. All we could do was look down and shake our heads. Looking back, I thought we had a pretty normal upbringing. My mom would give the shirt off her back to make sure her kids had what they needed. We would tell her sometimes to buy herself something when we went shopping, but she always said, "No!"

However, in the last few months, things began to change. My parents started arguing more, and soon, my dad moved out of the house. We tried to carry on with our lives as normally as possible. The Thursday before Good Friday, we had our Drama class performance. I remember being on stage and hearing my mother's laughter in the audience. It was my first time performing, and I loved every minute of it.

After the performance, we stopped at my aunt's house for a little while before heading home for the evening. My mom and I waited for my sister to get off work. Like any other night, we got ready for bed and said our good nights.

During the night, I was suddenly woken up by a familiar voice. Though I couldn't fully comprehend what was happening, I sensed urgency in the air. As I lay there, the voice grew louder. Then, in a jarring moment of clarity, I realized a shotgun was pointed directly at my face. I blinked a few times to focus, and that's when I saw him—my dad. He paced back and forth between my room and the hallway, unaware of what he was doing.

Panic set in as I quickly got up, walked to my desk, and grabbed my glasses. His voice was frantic, telling me we had to leave—immediately. I was confused, scared, and still trying to process everything, but I nodded and said, "Okay, just let me tell Mom I'm going with you." As I walked from my room toward my mom's room, a loud boom echoed through the house. In that moment, I felt an excruciating pain in my back and found myself staring at the green carpet beneath me.

My dad yelled for me to get up, but as I lay there, I realized something was terribly wrong. My upper body was flat against the carpet, but my legs felt as though they had sunk into a hole. I looked down—my legs were there, but I couldn't feel them at all. I told him I couldn't move. He kept screaming at me to get up, but then the sound of another gunshot pierced the air.

This time, I stayed still, silent. The television show *Rescue 911* flashed through my mind, and at that moment, I knew I had to play dead because if I moved again, he would probably kill me. After a few minutes of silence, I began to think that maybe, just maybe, he would believe I was dead.

It was then that I felt something cold and wet being poured over me— and throughout the entire house. My senses finally caught up with me, and I realized what it was *gasoline*. The fear was overwhelming, and my mind raced. Had he shot my mom and sister, too? Were they playing dead, like me? In the back of my mind, I thought, *If he lights the house on fire, I'll crawl to the bathroom window and try to jump out.* But then I heard him cut off the lights.

I attempted to move, and I froze when I heard him call my name. *Oh no*, I thought. *He heard me move.* My heart pounded, and I lay there, terrified, hoping he wouldn't shoot me again. Then, something seemed to shift in him. He paused, and the next words that came from his mouth were, "Do you want me to take you to the hospital?"

I looked up at him, my mind racing, and whispered, "Yes, please. I promise I won't tell anyone what happened." He carefully turned me onto my back and began dragging me through my mom's bedroom toward the living room. I could hear him rummaging around for the keys to my mom's car, and I felt each movement in my body—painful, slow, and disorienting. He pulled the car up to the front door and continued dragging me outside. My pajama pants started to slip off, and he tried to adjust them, but the pain was unbearable. I remember begging him, "Please don't leave me."

He managed to get me into the backseat of my mom's car, then ran back into the house to grab a blanket and cover me. I couldn't remember much of the drive to the hospital. All I knew was the pain—sharp and constant—and my dad's voice, asking me if I was okay.

When we finally arrived at the hospital, I remember him rushing in to get help, calling for nurses or staff to come with a gurney. They pulled me from the car, and as I looked up, I saw my dad's face. He looked at me, trying to reassure me, and said, "Everything's going to be okay." Those words felt like cruel irony, and I couldn't shake the confusion and terror of what had just happened.

That was the last time I ever saw or spoke to my dad. I was taken straight to the back of the hospital and into an exam room. There was so much commotion—doctors and nurses asking me what felt like a million questions. But I just kept repeating, "I don't know. I don't know what happened." I was always Daddy's little girl, and I remembered the promise I had made to him.

As they examined me, one of the doctors noticed I wasn't wearing any bottoms. They gently asked if I had been raped or molested. They knew I had a gunshot wound, but they were trying to determine what else had happened to me. I kept saying, "I don't know," over and over. Then finally, after several minutes, I motioned for the examiner to come closer. In a whisper, I said, "My dad."

I felt a wave of betrayal wash over me. Outside the room, I could hear a commotion in the hallway. I think they were questioning him, but then he got scared and ran. I kept telling them my address, pleading for someone to check on my mother and sister. I didn't know if they had been shot, too—if they were playing dead like I had—or if they were still alive. Someone had to go see about them.

At first, I was going to ask them to call my grandmother, but then I hesitated and said, "Please call my aunt." She arrived at the hospital hours later, though I don't know how long I had to wait. Eventually, I was taken into surgery and then placed in intensive care for several days.

I remember feeling drowsy, my mind clouded with medication and exhaustion. I kept asking my family, "Where are my mom and sister?" But no one would give me an answer.

Then, finally, I looked at my aunt and said, "They're dead, aren't they?"

She didn't respond, but I could see it in her face. That was all I needed to know.

My heart shattered.

What happened that night?

Could this really be my life?

Could my dad have truly killed my mother and sister and shot me?

I had to be dreaming… Someone please wake me up!

Later, I learned that after leaving the hospital, my father went to his brother's house and committed suicide.

The trauma was so severe that my mind began blocking certain things out as a way to survive. I couldn't even visualize what my family looked like. I started to wonder if I was losing my mind—how could I forget their faces? Had I really erased them from my memory?

My aunt showed me their obituaries, and I let out a sigh of relief. Those were the faces I could no longer visualize. I was grateful to see their pictures again, yet heartbroken at the same time.

I spent several days in the ICU, and once I was stable, they moved me to a regular room. While I was there, teachers, classmates, friends, and family came to visit me at the hospital in Oxford. When my teachers arrived, I immediately started worrying about school and my classwork. But they reassured me that it was the last thing I needed to focus on—I just needed to get better. I remained in the hospital for a couple of weeks until I had gained enough strength to begin rehab.

Rehab

Because I was so young at the time, I thought rehab meant learning how to walk again. I spent a couple of weeks in our local hospital before being transferred to a rehabilitation center in Tupelo. In hindsight, Tupelo might not have been the best place for rehab, but my family didn't want me to go too far away under the circumstances. I had the option to go to rehab in Atlanta, Georgia, or elsewhere, but my family chose Tupelo because it was just an hour away.

The hospital mostly focused on older patients and stroke victims, but I was fortunate to have a wonderful physical therapist who was dedicated to helping me with daily functions.

I had to learn everything all over again, and I had to do it while sitting down. I had to learn how to use a transfer board to get in and out of bed and even how to get into and out of a car. I also had to learn how to dress myself while sitting in bed, which was incredibly frustrating.

As a T5 incomplete spinal cord injury patient, I have limited trunk muscles. Every time I tried to put on my pants, I fell over in bed. Some days, I laughed at myself; other times, I cried.

An incomplete spinal cord injury means I still have some sensation but not the true feeling I once had in my upper body. I can feel someone touch my legs, and I can sense when my foot, leg, or bottom is hurting.

Before my injury, I didn't realize how much the core plays a role in posture, reaching for things, or even putting on clothes while sitting in bed. The little things I had once taken for granted were no longer automatic.

Not being able to move my legs or feel hot and cold was an odd and unsettling experience. At first, it frustrated me, but I was determined to figure it out—that's just my stubbornness showing through.

I even learned how to cook while sitting down. It was an interesting challenge. At first, I was scared because the stove was so close to my face and body that I feared I'd burn myself. The first thing I cooked was an egg.

I also learned how to use a reacher to grab items from top shelves and to put things above my head. Additionally, I had to practice pushing a wheelchair. While it may sound simple, it takes practice and technique. To turn, you have to know which wheel to grab in order to slow yourself down while pushing the other one. They had roped off a section of the rehab floor for us to practice rolling, turning, and maneuvering in different directions.

One memory that stands out is celebrating Mother's Day without my mom. I remember going to breakfast and all I could do was cry. The other patients were celebrating Mother's Day, and all I could think was that I was sitting there without my mother. I didn't know how to process it. In that moment, it hit me that my family wasn't with me anymore. They took me to a private room to eat my breakfast, and I screamed, **"It's Mother's Day, and I don't have a mother!"** It was a hard reality to face.

As I gained strength, I was able to go home for weekends during my rehab. It was nice to see my family, but it was also scary. We had to drive by my old house on the way to my grandmother's, and each time we passed, it filled me with anxiety and fear.

Once I got home, I was able to attend rehab a few times a week. I had the best physical therapist—she was honest with me from the start, admitting that she hadn't worked with many spinal cord injuries before. But she was willing to learn alongside me, and that meant everything.

She helped me with my transfers and even supported me as I stood on the parallel bars with braces. Her patience, encouragement, and determination made all the difference in my recovery.

New Normal/High School

When I left school, I was a typical eighth grader who walked; when I returned as a ninth grader, I used a wheelchair. I wasn't sure how people would react to seeing me so different. I wasn't comfortable with my own body, so I could only imagine what others would think when they saw me.

My family had purchased a van and modified it with a wheelchair lift. Sometimes, I felt like a queen as I was lowered out of the van, but other times, I just wanted to shrink because everyone would stare. At that time, my grandmother dropped me off at school along with my two younger cousins. The school suggested I ride the accessible (short) bus, but I was adamant about not feeling different, so I declined. It took several months for everyone to adjust to seeing me arrive at school, and eventually, the stares faded away.

I can honestly say everyone was welcoming and treated me the same. We had to make a few adjustments in my classrooms. The school was kind enough to provide rolling tables in all my classrooms so I could complete my work comfortably. However, the bathrooms were a different story. While the school had a few male students who used wheelchairs, there were no female-accessible bathrooms. They were very accommodating, though, and converted a bathroom in a newer building so that a nurse could meet me there and assist me when I needed help.

The school even allowed me and my two best friends to alternate between Mr. Buford's and Ms. Lauderdale's classrooms before first period, so I didn't have to sit in the gym with the other students. They tried to make everything as normal as possible, though I knew nothing would ever be quite the same.

I've always been a bit of a nerd in school. I would say my best friends and I were like the nerd, the cheerleader, and the athlete—together, we were a triple threat, balancing each other out. Where one was weak, the others would encourage or lift her up. We laughed, studied, and cried together throughout high school. Even when we argued, one of our teachers—who was Black—would talk to us afterward to remind us that we needed to support one another. She would say we had enough challenges in the world as young Black women; we didn't need to make it harder on each other.

In my junior and senior years, I was accepted into a math and science camp for students with disabilities in Seattle, Washington, on the campus of the University of Washington. This was the first time I met people who looked like me and had experienced trauma that resulted in using a wheelchair. I had never been in a room with so many people with various disabilities, including those with learning disabilities or who were blind.

Before we traveled to campus, the staff visited our homes to provide us with computers and internet access so we could communicate with one another. This was my first time flying and traveling out of state with a disability. Saying I was nervous would be an understatement, but I wanted to experience the world beyond Mississippi. It was also the first time I was seen as "normal" and not just a person in a wheelchair. I've always preferred to be seen for what I *can* do, not for what I can't.

At the camp, we took classes in math and science and had some fun downtime, like going to a Seattle Mariners baseball game.

As I mentioned, I've always been a nerd, and that didn't change just because I used a wheelchair. I still enrolled in honors and AP classes throughout high school, participated in field trips, and even joined the science fair. I was the "cool nerd" who was always involved in something. I was a member of the National Honor Society, Beta Club, French Club, and Student Council. I was also recognized in *Who's Who*, voted *Most Likely to Succeed*, inducted into the Hall of Fame, and graduated with special honors, ranking number four in my class.

I was never the type to dress up, so when it was time for senior prom, I was terrified. I had always been the pretty friend, but never the one the guys were interested in. So, I was pleasantly surprised when I was asked to prom.

My aunt made my prom dress, and my best friend's friend came over to do my makeup. For the first time in a while, I felt beautiful. My prom date picked me up, and of course, my aunt took a million pictures before we left. She even had to explain to my date how to put my wheelchair in the trunk and how I needed to get into the car. I was nervous but thankful that he treated me with respect, like any other lady. Two of my male classmates helped me get into the charter bus that took us to Memphis, where we boarded a riverboat for the prom. We laughed, danced, and had a wonderful time that night.

College

I honestly didn't know where I wanted to go to college—I just knew it wasn't Ole Miss. When you're born and raised in a college town, you want to experience something different as a young adult. I remember taking a road trip with one of my best friends, her mom, and my aunt to Southern Miss. It felt like the longest road trip of my life. But once we got there, I knew it wasn't the school for me. The campus had a lot of hills, and many of the buildings weren't wheelchair accessible.

I had a few friends applying to MS State, so I decided to apply, too. I was unsure about a major, but I loved math, and my aunt suggested accounting. I thought it was just about numbers—but boy, was I in for a rude awakening.

I took another college visit to MS State, and I was pleasantly surprised by the accessibility and accommodations they offered. I hadn't considered being a Bulldog before, but after touring several colleges, I realized that MS State was the most accessible one in Mississippi. My aunt was a little freaked out at first—she still saw me as her little girl and wanted me close to home. But after a long talk, she understood that this was something I needed to do for myself.

Move-in day as a freshman was both exciting and nerve-wracking. My aunts and cousins helped me move in, and I was fortunate to have a private room since there were only a limited number of accessible dorms. I stayed in the all-girls freshman dorm, Rice Hall. As we were moving in, I did get some stares because most people hadn't met someone in a wheelchair who was as independent as I was in going to college.

My freshman year, my classes were spread all over campus. I got a lot of calluses from rolling around. I even tried an electric wheelchair once—yes, just once! I felt so uncomfortable and out of control that I was afraid I'd fall out at any moment. I was thankful for the chair, but I never used it again.

I was lucky to have some wonderful hallmates during my college years. Some of the ladies were eager to help me when needed and even walked with me to class when our schedules allowed. One of the sweetest people I met my freshman year was Adrienne, who worked the front desk. We just started talking one day, and we hit it off right away. She was so kind and didn't mind taking me to stores or running errands. She looked past my wheelchair and treated me as a person—something I truly appreciated.

Sometimes, I feel like a burden when I ask people for help, especially with things like getting in and out of cars or needing extra space to store my wheelchair. Not everyone is willing to help, but Adrienne always was.

When I got to college, I realized I hadn't dealt with the trauma I'd experienced. I had buried it, moving on with life as best as I could. But as I met new people and listened to them talk about their parents, it made me miss what I didn't have. In normal conversations, people asked about my hometown, my major, and what my parents did, and I would have to tell them my parents were deceased. It wasn't their fault, but it made me feel depressed during my sophomore year, and I ended up seeking counseling.

Have you ever cried and couldn't stop? That was me. I had pushed my grief down for so long, thinking I was fine, but it caught up with me. I started staying on campus during breaks like Thanksgiving, avoiding home because I was struggling. Despite it all, I kept pushing forward, doing what I knew best—surviving.

College was different and being an accounting major was different, too. I had always been an A student, but suddenly, I was struggling to make C's. I'd call my aunt crying, and she would tell me that a C was passing and not to be so hard on myself. But I didn't understand why everything seemed to be going wrong. I spent all night studying for an accounting test, only to barely pass. I had always thought of myself as smart, but my grades didn't reflect that. It was discouraging.

I also didn't have much of a social life, as most of my time was spent studying or working on group projects. Looking back, I wish I had stressed less and enjoyed life more. But despite the pressure, I was able to join a few clubs: Black Student Alliance, the Association of Black Business Professionals, the Student Association, and, of course, Delta Sigma Theta, the best sorority around.

I'm grateful for all the people I met in college. It was a time of learning, growth, and showing others that I'm just like everyone else—I just do things differently. A special shout-out goes to my friend, Kerry, whom I met during my sophomore year. She became my sounding board and my outlet, seeing me for who I truly am. Kerry was always there for me, whether it was for a meal or a quick shopping trip to Tupelo.

First Job

Looking for a first job can be scary, especially for someone who has never worked a day in her life and uses a wheelchair. I submitted a few applications but received no callbacks. Two months passed before someone suggested applying at FNB (formerly First National Bank). To my surprise, I got a call back!

When the call came, I was both excited and nervous. The Vice President of Sales asked if I was interested in a teller position. I paused for a moment, cleared my throat, and explained that I used a wheelchair and wouldn't be able to see over the counter. Her response shocked me, she told me she would do some research and get back to me.

A few days later, she called again with good news. The bank had a shorter counter at the end of the teller line that they could convert into a teller station just for me. Shortly after, I went in for an interview and was hired! I had landed a full-time job, earning my own money. It wasn't a lot, but it gave me independence and the satisfaction of doing things on my own. It wasn't an accounting position, but hey, everyone has to start somewhere!

That first job taught me the realities of the workplace—the good, the bad, and the ugly. You don't always like the people you work with, but you still have to show up and do your job. I also learned that some people may feel threatened by you for reasons beyond your control. I had to remind myself to go to work, smile, do my job, and go home.

Thankfully, I never experienced anyone doubting my ability to do my work. However, customers sometimes stared once they realized I was in a wheelchair. Being a teller wasn't my favorite job—not because of the work itself, but because I couldn't use the restroom as freely as I needed to. With a spinal cord injury, bladder control isn't always predictable. There were times when I had to hold it because I couldn't leave my station in the middle of helping a customer. I even had to monitor what I drank to avoid accidents during the day.

Thankfully, that job only lasted eighteen months. God always places you where you need to be, even when you don't realize it. If I hadn't been working at FNB, I wouldn't have met the woman who offered me my next job. I ended up moving to the building right behind FNB to work for the county, where I stayed for the next eleven years!

Those years were some of the most rewarding and challenging times of my life. I had amazing mentors, coworkers, and supervisors who taught me valuable lessons about work ethic and leadership. I will always be grateful for Kelley, Lisa, Jamie, Stacie, and Joseph! I started that job as a young woman and grew into the person I am today because of the experiences I had working alongside them.

Support System

I am thankful for the family I have. I never received any special treatment just because I used a wheelchair—favoritism was the last thing I could expect from them. They treated me just like everyone else, joking with me and making me laugh.

I used to tell my aunt that if she made me mad, I would kick her. Without missing a beat, she would turn around and say, "Okay, do it! Let me see you move that leg!"

I remember one time when I fell out of my wheelchair in my bedroom. I called my aunt's name for help, and as soon as she walked in, she burst out laughing. She told me that I looked like a turtle stuck on the floor!

I love my family and the bond we share. Their humor, love, and support have shaped me in ways I will always cherish.

I have some of the best childhood, college, and adult friends a girl could ask for. Each one of them plays a unique role in my life.

I've never been the best at expressing my feelings or emotions, but my childhood friends just know me. They understand so much about me without me having to say a word, and for that, I am truly grateful.

My college friends got to witness me adapting to new environments, complaining about school, and trying to figure out life as a whole. They saw the struggles of young adulthood firsthand and stood by me through it all.

My adult friends—bless their hearts—have seen the pain and anxiety that come with unhealed wounds. They've watched me be the strong one, even when I probably wanted to break down and cry or question what life had in store for me.

I am not the same person I was in my teens or twenties. Life has a way of knocking you down but having a circle of friends to lift you up and offer words of encouragement makes all the difference.

Thank you! Thank you! Thank you—Kondra, Cecilia, Kerry, Erica, Shannon, and Kantress! I wouldn't have made it through life without you!

Let Go and Let God

God and I currently have a love-hate relationship, much like my relationship with my wheelchair. Yes, people tell you to pray about it and give it to God, but sometimes, those things are hard to do. I've been angry at God, and I wouldn't say I'm totally over it, but I'm starting to open up my heart to let Him in and heal me.

In my mind, it's easy to say that God is a healer and that He knows what's best for us. But then I find myself asking, *Why me, Lord? Why did You have to take away my entire family and leave me here?* These are not easy questions to ask nor are they easy to answer, but they are the thoughts that enter my mind.

The older I get, the more I miss my mom. I love my aunts and my grandmother, but there's nothing like a mother's love. I'll never feel that same unconditional love again. The older I get, the more I wish she was here so I could ask her thoughts on different situations that come up in my life.

Yes, God is our source and provider, but He also created therapists. I wish it still wasn't seen as taboo for people to seek therapy. Prayer and therapy can go hand in hand. A few years ago, I learned an important lesson from my therapist. I told her that, around Mother's Day, I would grieve and feel sad, but my feelings were cut off on Father's Day. I felt like I was betraying my mom and sister if I missed my dad. She told me that it was okay to grieve my father and the things he did. At that time, I couldn't separate the two.

I know my mother's side of the family probably has mixed feelings about my dad for what he did, and I know my dad's side of the family feels the exact same way. I'm learning that you can love a person but not agree with their actions. I can grieve the father that I knew and loved while also being angry about what he did on that day. Someone once told me; *Your dad was a good man; he just had a bad day and did a bad thing.*

Life must go on. I will continue to pray that God shows me my purpose through all of this trauma and that it wasn't in vain. I will never fully get over losing my family, but I've learned to cope with it.

No one can really explain grief. You can be having a good day, and suddenly, a song, an object, or a memory can hit you, making you feel that loss all over again.

I hope my story lets you know—you are not alone, and we can all rise above the concrete with the help of God.

About the Author

Shakethia Shaw, a trailblazing first-time author, joins forces with fellow empowering women with disabilities in a groundbreaking anthology. Hailing from Oxford, Mississippi, Shakethia's impressive academic credentials include a Bachelor's Degree in Accounting from Mississippi State University and an MBA from Belhaven University.

Shakethia's dual passions for numbers and highlighting the resilience of individuals with disabilities drive her daily life. When not immersed in finance or writing, she enjoys teaching Sunday School, word search puzzles, shopping, and cherishing time with loved ones.

An active member of the Oxford Alumnae Chapter of Delta Sigma Theta Sorority, Inc., and a devoted member of Union Hill MB Church, Shakethia embodies the spirit of service and leadership.

Through her contribution to the anthology, Shakethia aims to inspire readers, shedding light on the remarkable strength, perseverance, and potential of the disability community. Her story serves as a testament to the power of resilience and determination.

How to Connect with Shakethia:

Email: slshaw99@gmail.com
Instagram: @slshaw

Acknowledgements

In loving memory of Herbert, Samantha, and Forteshia Shaw—your memories will forever be etched in my heart. Though you may be gone, your love, strength, and legacy continue to shape me into the person I am today. I carry your spirit with me, and it guides me in all that I do.

To my remarkable aunts, Vivian Smith and Telisa Curry, and my wise and loving grandmother, Ruthie Mae Smith, I extend my deepest gratitude for being pillars of strength, guidance, and unwavering support in my life. Your influence has inspired me to persevere through life's challenges and obstacles.

To my entire family, church family, friends, mentors, and colleagues, I am profoundly thankful for your love, encouragement, and belief in me throughout the years. Your support has been a constant source of motivation, and I am humbled by your presence in my life.

A special thank you to Kebra Moore—for your push, guidance, and unwavering support. There were moments when I felt like quitting, but your encouragement helped me to keep pushing forward. I am truly honored that you chose me to be a part of this anthology.

To everyone who has contributed to my journey—I thank you from the bottom of my heart. Your collective love, support, and guidance have made me who I am today, and I am forever grateful. With love, gratitude, and appreciation!

www.ingramcontent.com/pod-product-compliance
Lightning Source LLC
Chambersburg PA
CBHW060451310726
48977CB00001B/400